A Ponderosa Resort
Romantic Comedy

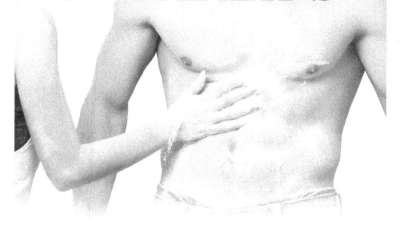

Chef
SUGARLIPS

USA Today Bestselling Author
TAWNA FENSKE

CHEF SUGARLIPS

A PONDEROSA RESORT ROMANTIC COMEDY

TAWNA FENSKE

ABOUT CHEF SUGARLIPS

Sean Bracelyn can whip up a saffron-laced lobster risotto in his sleep, but relationships? That's one recipe he hasn't nailed. Not that he has time, between launching a new restaurant and building a luxury resort with his awkwardly-blended family. But when his dream girl nearly knocks him unconscious with a dead turkey, it's all Sean can do to keep his eyes on the gazpacho and off Amber King's perfect curves.

Amber's done with guys propping her on a pedestal. Transforming her family's reindeer ranch into a country chic wedding venue is consuming enough, and the last thing she needs is an extra serving of love drama. So what is it about the stupid-sexy chef that gets her desires bubbling like a pot of hot spaghetti?

Keeping their distance is tough enough before Sean and Amber get tossed together by wacky weddings, lingerie mishaps, and a surly three-legged cat. When Sean's mom shows up to dish out huge helpings of family drama, a big secret threatens to spread faster than a kitchen fire.

Can Sean and Amber find the right blend of sugar and spice, or will love fall flat as a burnt soufflé?

ALSO IN THE PONDEROSA RESORT ROMANTIC COMEDY SERIES

- Studmuffin Santa
- Chef Sugarlips
- Sergeant Sexypants
- Hottie Lumberjack
- Stiff Suit
- Mancandy Crush (novella)
- Captain Dreamboat
- Snowbound Squeeze (novella—coming Jan. 17!)
- Dr. Hot Stuff (coming soon!)

For Kait Nolan.
Thanks for shoving me into the deep end.
The water's warm here, or maybe that's pee?

CHAPTER 1

"*P*icture a bunch of twinkle lights in those rafters, and the hay bales over there would be the edge of the dance floor."

I deliver my most charming smile to the bride and groom before zeroing in on the mother of the bride. She beams like I've handed her a puppy and a vodka-laced Frappuccino, and I'm positive I am currently her favorite person in this barn.

I have that effect on moms.

But it's the bride who needs convincing, so I turn back to her. Julia's blonde hair is arranged in a stylishly messy French twist, and her outfit is classic college-girl-approaching-the-threshold-of-real-life. I want to ask where she found her vintage Coach bag, but now's not the time.

"Did you get the Pinterest page I sent with those flowers in mason jars?" I ask.

"Yes," she says slowly, glancing around like she expects a farm animal ambush. "They'd be pretty with rose gold ribbon."

"Absolutely." I flick a hand toward the imaginary tables. "Picture them with little stargazer lilies. Or maybe early-season tulips. Those should be available this time of year."

Julia's blue eyes continue a survey of the space, and I know she's seeing it in her mind.

The rustic wine barrels spilling with wildflowers.

The cute chalkboard signs pointing people to her guest book.

The train of her gown gliding through a pile of fresh reindeer droppings.

The beast responsible for the droppings snorts and rubs her branchlike antlers on a post.

"Tammy won't be invited to your ceremony," I assure the bride and groom. "We keep the reindeer penned up during weddings."

Tammy the reindeer stamps a hoof and keeps banging her antlers on the post. She's due to lose them any day now, and I say a silent prayer it won't happen in the next five minutes.

"It's totally fine, honey," the mother of the bride assures me. "The whole point of doing a rustic, country-style wedding is having some flavor."

"We can certainly offer that." I turn back to the happy couple. "We're all about the quaint, country charm."

The groom—who's been mostly quiet up to this point—takes his bride's hand and studies her face as intently as she's watching Tammy. "What do you think, honey?" he says. "It has that homey, folksy vibe going for it."

Julia does an agreeable little head tilt, though I can't tell from her face if she thinks that's a good thing or a bad thing. "I guess rustic country chic is all the rage right now." She glances at me for affirmation. "I see a lot of that on Pinterest."

I nod like a bobblehead, grateful for the powers of Pinterest in backing up my business plan. "Did you see last month's cover of *Bride* magazine? Country chic is in."

The mother of the bride puts a hand on her daughter's arm. "Remember that episode of *Say Yes to the Dress* where they had those adorable burlap table runners and centerpieces with bright red apples in little metal tubs?"

Tammy the reindeer swings her antlers our direction, and I hold my breath. She knows that word, and she's poised to stomp over here and start snuffing at pockets for Honeycrisps. I focus very hard on using mental telepathy to beg my sister to come drag the blasted reindeer out of the barn.

But since Jade and I aren't telepathic, Tammy just stares.

"It's nice, I guess," Julia says, with roughly the same enthusiasm I'd use to describe the work gloves I bought last week.

"I think it's totally charming." The groom squeezes her hand, and I can tell he really means it. "My family would say it's exotic."

"Exotic." Julia frowns a little. "That's because they're from Manhattan. It's not exotic when you spent childhood summers mucking stalls."

"Now, honey." The mother of the bride puts an arm around her daughter's shoulders and smiles at me. "It's a hat tip to your heritage."

"A way to blend our lives together." The groom smiles, then lowers his voice just a touch. "And we are sort of in a hurry."

The look they exchange confirms what I guessed the second these two first called about pulling off a wedding in five weeks.

My own furtive glance at his Allen Edmonds shoes and Ralph Lauren slacks fills out the rest of the picture: East Coast boy from old money knocks up college sweetheart whose middle-class upbringing comes from cattle ranching instead of blue chip stocks. Opposites attract, etcetera etcetera, and graduation's close enough that no one will question a hasty spring wedding.

"How about I email you some figures and a link to another Pinterest board with a few ideas I think you might like," I tell them. "That'll give you some time to talk things over."

The mother of the bride hoists her leather bag a touch higher on her shoulder. "That would be lovely, dear. Can I also get you to send us some more suggestions for catering? None of the ones you mentioned were quite what we're looking for."

"We're foodies," the bride says, smiling as she shoots an

adoring look at the groom. "Our first date was at Le Bernardin in New York City."

"Not a problem," I tell them, which isn't totally true. Catering options are limited in Central Oregon, especially this time of year. "I'll make some calls and see what I can find."

"Wonderful," chirps the mother of the bride. "We'll be in touch."

The three of them shuffle toward the door, and the groom holds it open for his betrothed. As the barn door closes, the bride's voice carries back to me in a hushed half-whisper.

"It's too bad that Ponderosa Luxury Resort place isn't open yet. That would be perfect."

Damn.

Well, we knew there'd be some overlap between the rustic country-style weddings we're offering and the plans for hoity rich person weddings at the ranch-turned-luxury-resort down the road. It's to be expected. We even met with their marketing VP to make sure no one's stepping on anyone else's toes, but still.

I turn and trudge out the door and into the paddock where my sister is busy shaving mud balls off the hindquarters of a large reindeer steer.

"This week on *Lifestyles of the Rich and Famous*," I announce. "The glamorous world of reindeer ranching."

Jade rolls her eyes and snips another mud ball. "You want to give me a hand here?"

I grin and step close enough to plant a kiss behind the reindeer's left antler. "Hey, Harold," I say as Jade maneuvers an especially large glob of muddy fur. "Are you glad you don't have to wear the Donner harness and jingle bells anymore?"

"So happy that he gave himself a mud bath," Jade mutters. "How'd it go with the wedding couple?"

"Tammy was very helpful."

"Crap, sorry. I thought I had her penned in."

"It's fine, she was mostly charming," I say. "Pretty sure the couple's going to sign on for that date in five weeks."

"Shotgun wedding?"

"That's my guess.

"God bless failed birth control," my sister says.

"It'll keep these guys in beet pellets and hay when they're not earning their keep on the Christmas circuit."

Jade snips another mud ball as Harold tosses his massive antlers in dismay. "I'm impressed we're already booking this many weddings."

"I *am* kind of impressive, aren't I?" My cheeky quip earns me a snort from my sister and a grunt from Harold. I give him a scratch behind one enormous antler. "I think the catering thing is going to be an issue."

"How so?"

"No one's doing the farm-to-table thing everyone wants. Not this time of year, anyway. Options are limited for gourmet snobs."

"It's winter in a high-desert mountain town," she points out. "The only thing growing right now is juniper."

"Juniper's good for gin."

"What else would anyone need for a wedding?" Jade snips another mud ball and looks thoughtful. "You know, Brandon's cousin is a Michelin-starred chef."

"The one doing the restaurant stuff at *Ponderosa Luxury Ranch Resort?*"

I give the words the proper socialite sneer, even though we've mostly stopped mocking the neighbors for plunking down a rich person's resort in the middle of freakin' farm country. The fact that my sister is boning a member of their family might have something to do with that.

"Sean's a great cook," Jade says. "Maybe he has time for a side job, since they're not opening for another couple months."

"Huh." I like this idea. "Plus winter's slow for everyone," I add.

"And it could be a good way for them to get their name out there before they open." I rub my hands down the front of my jeans, eager to see if this could pan out. "I can give him a call and see what he says."

"Why don't you go in person," she says. "There's a turkey in the barn that I promised we'd deliver today."

"Alive or frozen?"

"Neither. It's that stuffed turkey grandpa shot when it attacked you in the driveway, remember?"

"The highlight of my toddlerhood." I kick at a dirt clod that looks like a misshapen penis, then feel bad when it crumbles to bits. "Why am I taking a taxidermied turkey to our new neighbors?"

"Some kind of photo shoot," Jade says. "Bree asked to borrow the turkey and one of Dad's old crossbows. They're thinking about offering turkey hunting trips for rich snobs who want to pretend they're outdoorsmen."

"Sounds like a good way for Percival to take an arrow through the hand."

"Percival?"

"That seems like a rich person's name, doesn't it?"

Jade looks thoughtful. "It's a good name for our next reindeer calf, actually."

I roll my eyes and turn toward the barn. "You're weird."

"Don't forget the turkey," she calls after me. "And the crossbow."

Words I never expected someone to yell at me when I graduated with honors from the U of O marketing department.

I trudge into the barn and locate the feathery beast, shuddering at the sight of it. I haven't seen the damn thing since third grade when I brought it to show-and-tell dressed in my mother's favorite bra and panty set. It was the first of several occasions my parents were asked to have a talk with me about the difference between appropriate and inappropriate public behavior.

I tuck the crossbow under my arm and spend a few moments figuring out the best way to carry the damn bird. The taxidermist posed it like it's poised to take flight, spreading its massive four-foot wingspan for full effect.

I settle for bear hugging it to my chest like the world's most awkward infant, and I heft it into the cab of the work truck for the five-minute drive to Ponderosa Luxury Ranch Resort.

For years, the place was the vanity ranch of an east coast billionaire who showed up a few times a year to play cowboy. It barely registered on my radar until the guy up and died, leaving the place to his adult kids, who've spent the last year quietly transforming it into a country-style luxury resort.

I have yet to see it in person. Running a reindeer ranch at Christmas doesn't leave much free time for tea and crumpets with the neighbors.

I pull through the massive wooden gates with the Ponderosa Luxury Ranch Resort logo spelled out in cast iron curlicue. The driveway is long and paved, which is the mark of extravagance this far out of town. Several massive, rustic-looking buildings line the drive, with signs announcing their intended purpose. There's the "Cedar Golf Club" and the "Aspen Springs Day Spa," and the "Tamarack Ballroom." I wonder if all those trees consented to having their names plastered on monuments to the wealthy.

I pull up in front of the biggest building of all, the one with a massive sign declaring it the Ponderosa Lodge and Luxury Suites. Beneath that is a smaller sign indicating it's also the home of Juniper Fine Dining. The whole building is designed to look like a vintage barn, but at ten times the size and with twenty times the windows. The water feature beside the front door probably cost more than my college education.

I park the truck and get out, then turn to grab my creepy welcome gifts. With the turkey hugged to my chest and the crossbow wedged awkwardly under one arm, I make my way along the paver-stone pathway to a set of massive glass doors that must be fifteen feet tall.

Hesitating a moment, I tap the bottom of the door with the toe of my boot. Not much of a knock, but the door swings open anyway. Automatic? Must be.

I step through it in a rush of light and sage-laced breeze, hoping I'm not walking right into someone's living room. The place isn't open to the public yet, so I'm not sure what to expect.

"Hello," I call out, squinting against the bright sunlight crashing down on me from all four sides. Good lord, it's going to cost a fortune to keep these windows clean. "Hellloooo?"

I blink hard, struggling to see anything through the flood of sunlight and the bundle of turkey feathers in my arms. There's a figure up ahead, a man. He's standing on a ladder, and as my eyes start to adjust, I realize "man" might be an understatement.

The dude is ripped. Broad shoulders, rounded biceps, and a build that could land him on the cover of *Men's Fitness*. The scruff on his face is the color of toasted cinnamon, and the hand that grips a screwdriver is the size of a dinner plate. His hair is sandy and tousled like someone's just run her fingers through it.

My fingers twitch at the thought of being that someone.

He turns and squints my direction, blinded by the force of the solar explosion gushing from the windows around me. As he blinks against the flood of light, I get a good look at his eyes. Good Lord, the color. Not just green, but a deep, shimmery bottle-green like glass glinting in the sun.

My mouth goes dry, and I stand there like an idiot while the guy gapes at me in silence.

"Holy shit," he says.

And then he passes out.

CHAPTER 2

SEAN

*F*or the record, I didn't faint.

Okay, I got rattled when I saw this angelic silhouette in the doorway, feathered wingtips arching toward opposite windows and dark hair shimmering like a sunlit halo.

Blame it on the fact that my sister made me binge-watch *Touched by An Angel* last week on the anniversary of our dad's death. Or hell, blame the fact that I've been sleeping like shit the last couple nights.

The point is, I know damn well there's not an actual angel in my foyer. That doesn't change the fact that I'm lying here on the floor beside the bar wondering what the hell just happened.

"Oh my God, are you okay?"

The angel sprints through the dining room and falls to her knees beside me, dropping a large turkey next to my head. I blink to clear my vision, pretty sure I'm seeing things.

When I spot the crossbow in her hands, I'm sure of it. "It's not a harp."

She stares down at me and bites her lip. "I think maybe you have a head injury." She sets down the crossbow and pulls an iPhone from the back pocket of her jeans, and I order myself not to notice the way the faded denim hugs her backside. "Hang on, let me call—"

"No." I struggle to sit up and catch her wrist before she hits the final 1 in 911. "Really, I just lost my balance. I'm fine."

Her head tips to one side as she studies me. "Actually, you do look fine." Her cheeks pinken the tiniest bit. "I mean—your pupils aren't dilated or anything, and you're not bleeding. Are you sure you don't have any internal injuries?"

"I promise, I'm okay." More than okay, since I'm still holding her wrist, which is warm and soft and fluttering with the fastest little hummingbird pulse. I should probably let go. "You're Amber."

The angel blinks at me. "How did you know that?"

I release her wrist and scrub a hand over the back of my head, confirming there's no blood. I'll have one helluva goose egg tomorrow, but that's the least of my concerns. "I remember you from a long time ago," I tell her. "I was eight, I think."

"Eight?"

"Yeah. So—nineteen years ago?"

"And you remember *me*?"

"I was visiting my dad here at the ranch that summer." I lean back against the wall, recalling the details of that meeting more acutely than I probably should. "You came over with your mom, looking for a pig that escaped."

The look on her face suggests she's back to questioning how hard I hit my head. "You remember that?"

What can I say? The pretty, brown-eyed girl with the sweet smile and dark waterfall pigtails made an impression.

"We met one other time," I tell her. "Well, *met* isn't the right word. You got caught skinny dipping in my dad's pond? It was your eighteenth birthday party, I think."

And the highlight of my summer as a twenty-year-old college kid standing on the back porch of my dad's ranch house wondering if there was some way to extend my week-long semi-annual visits to—well, an eternity.

Which is sort of what I've gone and done.

The memory of Amber with water streaming from her hair and moonbeams spotlighting her bare shoulders leaves me dizzy, and I consider lying down on the floor again.

She must see something alarming in my expression, because she clutches my arm and stares into my eyes. "Can you tell me your name? Or wait—how many fingers am I holding up?"

I smile, touched by her concern. "Sean. Sean Bracelyn. I'm one of the owners here."

"Oh. You're the chef?"

"That's me." I try not get too excited that she knows who I am.

Her forehead is still creased with a frown. "Are you sure I don't need to call anyone? An ambulance or maybe Bree?"

The thought of my sister storming in to tell me what a dumbass I am has me clambering to my feet in a hurry. I pull Amber up with me, not wanting to leave her sitting on the floor next to a dead turkey.

"What's with the bird?" I ask.

"My sister asked me to bring it."

"Because showing up with a plate of cookies is cliché?"

She laughs and shakes her head. "Your sister wanted it for some photo shoot. Don't worry, it's stuffed. I didn't just drop a freshly-killed animal on your floor."

"Too bad. I've got a killer recipe for spatchcocked turkey with anise and orange."

"Spatch—what?"

"Spatch*cocked*," I say, putting a regrettable emphasis on the last syllable. "It's where you lay it out flat with its legs spread wide and the breast—you know what? Never mind."

Christ, I need a do-over. It's not every day a guy comes face to face with the girl he's had a crush on since he wore Batman Underoos. I rake my fingers through my hair and try again.

"Let me start over," I say. "I promise to give the creepy dead turkey to my sister on your behalf."

"And the crossbow."

"Of course."

"I think it has something to do with a turkey hunting promotion."

"Or my sister's just weird," I say. "I wouldn't rule it out."

Amber laughs, and I get my first close-up look at the most adorable dimples I've ever seen. They're perfectly symmetrical, and the way she tosses her head back when she laughs makes me wonder what it would feel like to have all that hair spilling across my bare chest as she leans over me and—

For the love of Christ, knock it off.

I clear my throat. "Can I offer you a drink? The soda machine isn't hooked up yet, but we've got Perrier, Pinot Noir, an unoaked Chardonnay, a couple kinds of craft beer, a full bar..."

I stop there and cross my fingers she doesn't think I'm trying to get her drunk. She's smiling, so I don't think she's feeling threatened, but how would I know? I've fantasized about Amber King for years, but she's basically a stranger.

"Sure," she says. "I actually wanted to talk to you about something, so maybe we can sit down?"

"Hang on, let me grab us some snacks."

I hustle around the bar and shove through the doors to the kitchen. I've been doing my own dry-cured meats, so I slice up a little capicola, a few thin sheets of prosciutto, a bit of hard salami.

My phone buzzes from the cubby next to the fire extinguisher, and I steal a glance at the screen.

Mother.

Not mom, not mommy. *Mother.* That's how she's logged in my phone, which tells you everything you need to know about our relationship.

I spot the word "emergency" in the first few lines of her text message, but since her last so-called emergency was an urgent need to know how to spell the word "unencumbered," I ignore it and focus on assembling the best damn charcuterie tray ever.

I add a dab of pâté and grab a handful of pistachios, plus some of those Castelvetrano green olives I just got from Italy. I fill a small ramekin with whole-grain mustard and another with fig preserves before grabbing some baby dills for a little tart crunch.

I arrange the whole thing on one of the olivewood cheese boards my brother and I have spent the last week carving, then grab a bottle of Willamette Valley Pinot Noir and two glasses. Abandoning my phone in the kitchen, I start toward the door, then curse under my breath. I turn and grab the damn thing and shove it in my pocket, feeling it buzz with an incoming message as I head toward the dining room.

Amber's still standing right where I left her, one hand resting lightly on our hammered copper bar. She looks up as I push through the doors, and her eyes go wide as nickels.

"Holy crap," she says. "When I say I'm throwing together a snack, it means I'm dumping chips in a bowl. Maybe salsa if I feel fancy."

"I'm a chef," I tell her. "I can put together a charcuterie tray in my sleep."

"I'm a marketing geek and a reindeer rancher," she says. "So if you need crap shoveled one way or another, I'm your girl."

I hate how my heart stutters with those three words. *I'm your girl.* She didn't mean it that way, and we've only just met. But I can't stop thinking about what that would feel like.

"Come on," I tell her. "Let's have a seat in the dining area."

I lead her to one of the live-edge juniper tables near the window overlooking the mountains. As I set the tray down in the center, Amber stops to stroke one bark-edged curve.

"This is incredible," she says. "Did you get these at that Amish shop in town?"

I take a seat on one of the leather-backed chairs. "Nah, my brothers and I harvested timber off the east side of the property.

Brandon helped, too. We've been slowly building one table at a time for about eight months."

"You made this?" she shakes her head and takes a seat beside me. "A chef, a woodworker, and a resort owner."

"Sounds like the setup for a bad joke." I grab the wine bottle and hold it up. "I hope you don't mind, I went with the Pinot."

She leans in to peer at the label, and it takes everything in my power not to steal a glimpse down the v-neck of her sweater.

"Ooh, that's one of my favorite vineyards," she says. "Dundee Hills, right?"

"Right." Be still my heart, she knows wine. Did I mention I'm pretty sure she's my dream girl?

I uncork the bottle and tip a couple tablespoons into one of the glasses. Then I shove the cork back in the bottle and shake the crap out of it for about thirty seconds. "Old vintner's trick," I tell her. "It's a good way to aerate a wine fast when you don't have time to decant."

I hope I don't sound like a pretentious snob. I hope the fact that I can wield a chainsaw as well as a carving knife helps rub off some of my prep-school varnish.

The smile she gives me looks genuine as she plucks an olive out of the small dish on the edge of the tray. "Your wife or girl-friend or whatever—she must love this," she says. "Having a personal gourmet chef twenty-four seven?"

Hello. Was that a probe at my marital status, or just an entrée to conversation? Or maybe she's wondering if I'm gay.

"I'm not," I say, probably a little too quickly. "Married or in a relationship or anything. I was engaged once—to a woman—but I've actually never been married, so—"

Fuck. What the hell is wrong with me?

I clear my throat. "I cook for my family all the time, so I guess they're the ones reaping the benefits."

"Lucky them." She smiles and takes a small sip of the wine I've just poured into her glass. Then she plucks a thin slice of baguette from the tray and sets to work loading it up with capicola and salami with a little mustard. I watch, admiring her enthusiasm as she tops the whole thing with a little nugget of cave-aged gouda and takes a bite.

"God, this is amazing," she says around a mouthful. "I missed lunch, so you just saved my life."

"My pleasure."

"How did you end up out here, Sean?" she asks when she's done chewing. "You're from the East Coast, right?"

"Connecticut," I answer, wondering how much she's heard through the grapevine. Amber's sister is hot and heavy with my cousin, Brandon. I know how news travels in normal families, so I figure she's heard at least parts of the story.

"My dad was, uh—" I hunt around for an adjective that's not "bastard" or "cheating asshole."

"From considerable means?" Amber supplies.

"There you go." I grab a hunk of salami off the tray, not bothering with the bread. "He was this billionaire investor who had fantasies of being a good ol' boy. Came out to Oregon and started buying up land like he was collecting baseball cards. That's how he met my mother, actually."

"Your mom's from Central Oregon?"

"No, but her grandparents had a place here. Their original homestead is part of this acreage."

"No kidding? So you have roots here."

"More or less," I say, not wanting to go too far down the rabbit hole of discussing my mother. "Anyway, my dad had a house built and bought a bunch of horses and hired a buttload of ranch hands to run the place. He'd come out a few times a year to do his rhinestone cowboy thing. Sometimes he'd bring one of us."

"You and your siblings?"

I nod and wonder if she's picturing us as one big happy family unit. "We—uh—all had different mothers," I say. "My sister and my brothers and me."

"Oh." Amber nibbles the end of a tiny pickle and looks thoughtful. "You and Bree look so much alike."

"We all do," I tell her. "Me, Bree, Mark, James, Jonathon—"

"Wait, how many siblings do you have?"

I shrug and stab a spreader into the pâté. "A lot."

"And you all grew up together?"

"God, no. It wasn't like some sort of weird cult thing with all the sister wives together. My dad just liked to get married."

"And divorced?"

I snort and reach for a slice of baguette. "He probably didn't enjoy that part as much. His exes tended to be—*displeased.*"

Including my mother, but there's no point bringing that up. There's probably no point bringing up any of this, so I have no idea why I'm yammering on like a kindergartener giving his life story on the first day of school. I'm not usually such an open book with women or—well, anyone.

Amber doesn't say anything right away, but she looks thoughtful. Or maybe she's just hungry. She isn't shy about diving right into the food, and I love that she's not picking at it like a perpetually-starved supermodel.

"I'm sorry for your loss," she says. "Your dad, I mean."

"Thank you. We weren't close." I clear my throat. "Anyway, after he died and we inherited this place, my sister and brothers and I decided to do something different with it."

I'm annoyed with myself for droning on about my life and not asking a damn thing about her. I reach for a hunk of salami, but she has the same idea. Our hands collide, and we end up doing this awkward fist-bump.

"Whoops, sorry," I say over the audible crack of knuckles.

"No, I'm sorry. Did I get you with my ring?"

She turns her hand over, showing a stunning golden gem in a silver setting. The stone is big and rounded, and a glint of sunlight catches it just right to show a tiny insect trapped inside.

"That's beautiful," I tell her.

"Thanks. My grandpa gave it to me. Amber for Amber, I guess." She smiles, but there's something wistful in it. A sadness that tells me grandpa might be playing poker with my old man on the other side of the pearly gates.

That's assuming my dad qualified for entry. I have my doubts.

"So did you always want to run a reindeer ranch?"

She laughs and shakes her head. "No, my sister is the animal nut. I'm crazy about them, too, but she's the one who went to vet school and runs that side of the business."

"And you do the marketing?"

"That's right," she says. "Finding ways to make us profitable year-round instead of just when people want to show up and get their picture taken with Rudolph. Which leads me to why I'm here, actually."

"Reindeer photography?"

She smiles and takes a small sip of her wine. "Nope, I'm talking about what we do the rest of the year—weddings."

"Right, the country wedding thing? My sister mentioned it." I swirl the wine in my glass, wondering if I'm the only one feeling like this is a date.

"We're doing more of a rustic wedding thing," she says. "Catering to the local crowd."

"And we get the rich assholes who fly in for an exotic, old-West destination wedding?"

"Your words, not mine." Amber grabs another piece of bread. "I wanted to find out if you had any interest in catering a couple weddings between now and then. It could be a good promotional opportunity if you—"

"I'm in."

She blinks. "What?"

I suppose I should have played hard to get? Too late for that.

"I'm in," I repeat, grabbing a hunk of smoked cheddar. "I've done tons of weddings. Piece of cake. Well, I don't do cakes, but I'm game for the rest."

17

Jesus, Sean, shut up. Take the eagerness down about twelve notches.

But Amber just looks bemused. "You didn't give me a chance to give you my hard sell," she says. "I had all this persuasive evidence lined up to present to you."

"Oh, by all means." I lift my wineglass and gesture for her to continue.

"Okay, um—well, there's visibility," she says. "Everyone's buzzing about the new luxury ranch in town, but no one knows much about you. This is a good way to get your business name out there."

"Our business plan is aimed at vacationers from out-of-town," I point out. "I'm not sure how much local marketing we need."

"Ah, but locals might come out for the dining, right?"

"Definitely," I say. "Though we won't be doing offsite catering, so we don't really want to advertise that."

Amber frowns and drums her fingertips on the table. "Okay, well it's a good chance for you to interact with community members."

"I'm not really much of a people person," I admit. "The human interaction stuff is more my sister's scene."

"Um, okay." She presses her lips together. "I'd tell you it's a good chance to make a little extra money before you open, but something tells me money's not an issue."

I clear my throat. "It's not a real motivator."

Amber stares at me. "You've just shot down every persuasive argument I made," she says. "Do you take back your offer to do it?"

"Nope." I sip my wine and steal a look at the mountains. The sun is starting to drop behind them, casting a pinkish alpenglow on the landscape. I look back at Amber and my heart twists. "I'm still in."

"So—why?"

I hesitate, wondering if I should be honest or bullshit her.

Honesty. Bullshit was your dad's game.

"I'm a sucker for brown eyes," I admit. "And I like your smile."

She's taken aback. "Oh. Well." She presses her palms against the table and looks down at her hands like she's trying to identify them as part of her body. When she looks up at me again, her expression is unreadable. "I'm not really dating right now. My last relationship ended badly, and I'm really focused on work right now, so—"

"Amber, it's fine," I assure her. "I'm appreciating your company, not naming our future children."

She nods, but looks uncertain. Her hands rest on the table, and she twists her fingers into a complicated knot. "I—uh—have sort of a weird track record with men," she says. "Being someone's hood ornament or trophy or whatever instead of holding out for respect."

"If it helps, I respect the hell out of you," I tell her. "Even before you showed up with a dead turkey and a crossbow and knocked me unconscious."

She laughs as her cheeks pinken just a little. "Sorry about that. And I'm sorry for dumping all this on you. I've dated a lot of bullshit artists, and you don't seem like one."

"Thanks."

"I'm sure you're a totally nice guy."

"Mostly."

Her expression is the same one I expect she'd wear if I told her I have Santa and the Pope making bruschetta in my kitchen, but I decide to let it drop. The girl clearly has some trust issues. If we're going to be friends, it'll take more than a charcuterie tray to win her over.

"I should go." Amber stands up fast, nearly toppling her chair. "I need to get back to the ranch for feeding time."

I get to my feet more slowly, not quite sure what just happened. "So you'll be in touch about the wedding thing?"

"Oh. Yes. Um, here—let me add you to my contacts." She pulls out her phone and flutters her thumbs over the screen, keying in my name. "What's your number?"

I rattle it off, and she types in the digits, then taps the screen. As my butt begins to vibrate, she nods in confirmation. "There. Now you have me in your phone."

I pull it from my pocket, ignoring the alert indicating I have five missed calls from my mother. I tap to answer Amber's call, doing my best to keep a straight face. "Hello?"

She grins at me, but plays along. "Hey, is Sean there?"

"Speaking."

"Sean, this is Amber."

"Amber who?"

Her eyes dance as her smile widens. "Amber King. I was wondering if you'd be willing to stop by my ranch tomorrow between five and six. You can take a look at the space and we can talk more about the wedding."

"I'm going to need to look at my calendar. Can you hold, please?"

"Certainly."

I pull the phone from my ear and hold it against my chest. Amber gives me a curious look.

"It's a bad idea to seem too available," I whisper. "My sister told me that."

"Ah." Amber smiles and nods. "Good thinking," she whispers back.

I bring the phone back to my ear. "Amber?"

"Yes?"

"Yeah, I can do tomorrow evening. Want me to bring dinner?"

"Dinner?"

"Sure. Some samples of wedding food you can taste test."

"Oh, that's an awesome idea. Yes, please."

"It's a date, then." I click off, oddly bummed to end the call. I could keep flirting with her like this all evening.

No, we're not flirting. It's just professional banter. We've made that clear. I shove my phone into my pocket and turn toward the door. "Come on. I'll walk you out. I need to go chop firewood anyway."

She follows me toward the lobby, trailing just a few steps behind me. I get the sense she's hesitating, and I wonder if she wasn't really serious about leaving.

"Sean, wait."

I turn around fast. Too fast, since Amber runs right into me. I grab her arms without thinking, not wanting her to fall. Her hands go to my chest, and I'm not sure if it's a block or a grope. She tilts her head back and looks at me, eyes widening just a little.

I get this crazy sense she's going to kiss me. I hold my breath, wondering what the hell is happening. Her lips part, and she looks up at me with dizzying heat in those brown eyes. I don't move, determined not to fuck this up.

"I—um—" She licks her lips, eyes still fixed on mine. Her palms stay pressed to my chest, and I'm still holding her arms, so I'm a little mind-whacked from all this contact.

Her throat moves as she swallows, and her palms skid slowly down my chest. It's the softest caress I've ever felt, so gentle I'm not even sure that's what it was.

"Damn," she whispers, shaking her head.

When she raises her gaze to mine again, my heart lodges thick in my throat. I know I should say something, but I'm not sure what. "Amber—"

Bree's voice bursts through the doors. "Hey, Sean, where's my turkey?"

Amber and I spring apart like a pair of cats hit with a squirt bottle. My sister shoves her dark curls off her forehead gives me a look that says she knows damn well she just interrupted something.

But we're Bracelyns, so we're going to pretend it didn't happen.

"Hey, Amber," Bree says, her expression offering only the faintest flicker that she knows something's up. "I didn't know you were here. Jade called and said you had my turkey?"

"Yes, absolutely." Amber nods, avoiding my eyes. "I left it next to the bar, right beside the crossbow."

"Excellent." Bree grins. "You ladies were the first ones who came to mind when I thought of where to get a stuffed turkey."

"Glad to help." Amber looks back at me. "So I'll see you tomorrow? For the meeting. The catering thing, I mean."

"Definitely." I do my best to match her oh-so-professional tone. "I can bring some sample menus, too."

Amber's gaze slides back to Bree, and I can tell she wants my sister to know there's no hanky panky happening. Nothing but a business meeting. "Perfect."

I keep a straight face, determined to go along with that. To pretend what just happened between us wasn't the hottest near-miss kiss of my life.

"I'm looking forward to it," I add, my voice cracking only a little.

CHAPTER 3

"*G*od, I'm such a dumbass," I mutter.

My sister glances up as I stomp into the kitchen. It's not the first time I've greeted her like this, but should it bother me that she doesn't look surprised?

"What happened?" Jade asks.

I love that she phrases it that way. Not "what did you do?" or "who'd you grope now?"

Not that she'd have any reason to suspect I accidentally manhandled our neighbor.

I slump onto one of the barstools and run a hand over the smooth concrete countertop. We built it when we started remodeling our childhood home together, and it's still one of my favorite parts of the house. Jade is using a heart-shaped cookie cutter on a big sheet of sugary white dough, and I reach across the counter to swipe a nibble off one edge.

"Stop that," she says, slapping my hand away. "Make yourself useful and frost that batch over there."

I glance at the end of the counter to see a bajillion naked sugar cookie hearts on the cooling rack. "Did you get junk-punched by Cupid, or are these upside-down asses?" I flip one over and wiggle it like Beyoncé doing a booty shake.

My sister rolls her eyes and shoves a few tubes of icing at me. "They're for the residents at Brandon's Dad's place. I'm trying to spread some cheer."

"Ah." I feel bad about mocking treats meant for dementia patients, so I uncap one of the frosting tubes and set to work making the most cheerful damn cookies on the planet.

"So what happened?" Jade asks, jogging me back to the reason I'm here.

"Oh. I, um—might have almost kissed Sean."

My sister drops the cookie cutter and stares at me. "Come again?"

"I didn't mean to," I insist as I squeeze a thick squiggle of pink icing onto a cookie. "I explained how I'm not really dating right now and that it's important to have a professional relationship, and then I sort of stumbled into him as I was leaving, and when he caught me—"

"—you decided to thank him by polishing his tonsils with your tongue?"

"No! I said I *almost* kissed him." I sigh and focus on making artful flourishes of frosting. "Then his sister showed up."

I can't help feeling disappointed about that part. About what might have happened if Bree hadn't walked in. Would Sean have kissed me like I wanted him to, or would he have looked down at me pawing his chest like a hungry raccoon and said, "Lady, what is your deal?"

What *is* my deal? For crying out loud, I'd just finished telling him I wasn't interested. Mixed signals much?

I grit my teeth and reach for another cookie, determined to put this faux pas behind me.

"Huh." Jade looks thoughtful, not judgey, which is a relief. "You've got good taste, I'll give you that. Sean's hot. I've only met him a couple times, but he seems like a nice guy."

"He *is* a nice guy, which is the last thing I need right now."

Jade doesn't say anything to that, which is probably because she knows. She knows damn well how hard I've been trying to move beyond my image as the boy crazy baby sister with a parade of guys lining up at the door and a reputation for choosing the worst possible one.

"Chin up," Jade says as I set aside a decorated cookie and reach for another. "Even if you did grope him, I doubt he was too upset about it. He's probably posting to Facebook about how he got felt up by Flawless Amber."

"Ugh." I know she's teasing, but the last thing I need right now is a reminder of that stupid nickname. "Thank God he didn't go to school around here."

"It's a small town," she points out. "Maybe he's heard."

"I'm guessing the Bracelyn family has better things to talk about than our high school yearbooks."

"Let's hope." Jade turns to shove a tray of cookies in the oven, and I reach for another unfrosted one. At the rate I'm going through pink icing, we're going to need another batch.

"So did you get Sean to do the weddings?" she asks. "I mean before you stuck your tongue down his throat?"

"I told you, I didn't actually kiss him. I hardly even groped him."

"*I hardly even groped him.*" Jade grins. "We'll put that on your headstone."

I sigh and pick up a tube of white icing, adding a little fringe to my creation. "Why did you bring up that stupid Flawless Amber thing, anyway?"

"I had lunch with a couple vet techs who volunteered for the spay and neuter clinic," she says. "They were in your grade."

"And they mentioned it?"

She shrugs. "You're memorable, I guess. Not every girl has a half-page color photo in her school yearbook that makes her look like a freakin' supermodel."

"I still want to kill the yearbook staff," I mutter.

I know that's a lame thing to let bother me, and there are worse things than being voted Miss Congeniality. Worse than being captain of the soccer team, class president, and the only chick to magically survive puberty without zits. Tons of kids had it way rougher than I did, and I'm sure as hell not complaining.

But there's something about being stuck on a pedestal that makes people want to knock you off.

Or makes boys want to knock boots with you, which isn't ideal when you're looking to be more than a notch on someone's bedpost.

Jade looks down at my frosted masterpiece and frowns. She turns one of the cookies around to face her. "Did you seriously just make a dozen vagina cookies?"

I finish piping white pubic hair around the edges of the pretty pink frosting labia and set it on the plate. "Technically, they're vulvas. Not vaginas."

"You're not serious." She picks up the cookie I've just finished and lifts one eyebrow. "White pubic hair?"

"They're mostly senior citizens," I point out. "I thought they'd be cheered by the familiar."

My sister sighs and picks up another cookie, this one done in hues of tan and peach. What? I'm encouraging racial diversity.

"Remind me to be more specific with my instructions next time," Jade mutters.

"You said *cheerful*," I point out. "If vulva cookies don't make people smile, I don't know what will."

"I am not taking frosted genitals to my future father-in-law and his friends."

"Fine." I snatch the cookie back. "I'll make it a flower." A Georgia O'Keeffe flower, but still a flower. "Or we can save these ones for dessert tonight, since it's your turn to do dinner. That reminds me, I have a surprise for tomorrow night."

"Tomorrow?"

"I know it's my turn to cook, but Sean offered to bring dinner. Wedding food. Sort of a tryout, I guess."

Jade's expression turns regretful. "I have plans tomorrow." She gets this funny little moony smile on her face, and I know before she speaks a word that she's getting together with her fiancé. "Brandon got us tickets to see the Wailin' Jennys at the Tower Theatre. I'd really like to go."

"Oh. No, you should definitely go."

And she'll definitely end up staying at Brandon's place, which would normally be fine.

But it means I'll be all alone with Sean. All alone with those bedroom eyes and yummy facial scruff and broad shoulders and sex-rumpled hair. I set down the tube of frosting and practice sitting on my hands so I'm not tempted to grab him.

"It'll be fine," I tell her. "No problem. I'll totally behave myself."

Like the good sister she is, Jade does her best not to look dubious.

I'm dubious enough for the both of us.

* * *

I CHANGE outfits four times before I'm finally disgusted with myself and settle on gray skinny jeans with boots and a flowy pink sweater. It's feminine and unassuming, and totally says "professional" and not "I want to jump you."

At least I think it does.

I second guess myself when I throw open the front door and Sean does a double take. He's gentleman enough to snap his gaze from my boobs to my eyes in under a second, but not so gentlemanly that he avoided the boob check in the first place.

I shouldn't like it, but I do.

"Something smells yummy," I say.

"What? Oh—that's probably me."

I cringe, realizing he's not holding any food and I totally just sniff-ogled the neighbor. "Awkward," I mumble, which earns me a laugh.

"I just meant I probably smell like food," he says. "I've been in the kitchen all day."

"I promise I don't usually greet my houseguests by sniffing them." Or by gawking at them with my mouth half open. The man looks fine in black jeans tailored to his delicious posterior and a dark green wool coat that catches the green in his eyes.

Stop staring. Stop sniffing. Just act like a normal human.

"Come on in," I tell him. "Wait, do you need help bringing in food?"

"Everything's in the car," he says. "It's packaged up and should be fine for a little bit. I was hoping maybe I could see the venue before it's dark?"

"Good idea. I'll grab my coat."

I shrug into an oversized down parka and debate swapping out my favorite leather Frye boots for rubber muckers. The weather's been dry all week, so I take my chances on cute boots and mud-free trails.

"The barn's heated, but the path out there isn't," I tell him as I locate my hat and gloves. "In case you're worried about food temperature or brides freezing to death in strapless gowns."

"I wasn't worried. I figured you guys know what you're doing."

"Let's hope so."

I finish pulling on my gloves and push open the door, making sure to flick on the porch light. I consider grabbing my snub nose pistol from the gun safe, but decide against it. We've had no cougar sightings lately, and it's still light out. Besides, toting a weapon isn't the second impression I want to give a guy whose first impression of me involved a head injury and a crossbow.

I step into the cool early evening and shove my hands into my pockets. The air is cool and crisp and smells like sage and bitterbrush. It's too early in the season for crickets or frogs, but a nighthawk screeches somewhere in the distance.

Sean falls into step beside me. "So, uh—I hear you had a bit of an issue out here last month."

I look at him, wondering if he read my mind about the gun. If he knows why the thought crossed my mind at all. It's a small town, and secrets are tough to keep. "You mean the fact that I held my ex-boyfriend at gunpoint after he tried to burn down our barn?"

Sean looks startled. "I was talking about the cougar attack. One of your reindeer got hurt?"

"Oh. That." I clear my throat, feeling like an idiot. "Yeah. That was Randy. He's doing great now."

"I'm glad." He pauses. "I heard about the other thing, too. The guy's in jail, right?"

"Right." Chalk up another awesome choice to Amber King. "The whole thing is kind of embarrassing."

"How so?"

I glance at him, tall and broad and solid beside me on the footpath. Our breath comes in frozen, puffy clouds, and I take my time answering. "I guess I feel like an idiot for not knowing," I tell him. "For thinking he was a devoted boyfriend instead of a psycho jerk."

He shakes his head and kicks a pebble off the path. "That's on him, not you. It wasn't your fault you trusted a guy who turned out to be an asshole."

"Thanks." I've heard that before, of course. From my sister and mom and pretty much everyone who knows what happened.

Doesn't make me feel better, but I appreciate that people try.

We've reached the barn and, hopefully, the end of this topic. "Here we are," I announce a little too cheerfully. I push open the door and flip on the lights, breathing in the sweet scent of hay. "Ignore the mess. We were just organizing some of the Christmas stuff."

"Including the reindeer?"

"What?" I swing my gaze to the other side of the barn. "Oh, that's Vixen. Irene, I mean. We stopped using the stage names in January."

"Stage names?"

"They all have holiday alter egos." Irene trots over and snuffs at my pockets, looking for treats. I scratch behind her left ear, and she leans into me. "She went into heat this morning, so we're keeping her in here for a few days. She's—uh—aggressively lovey right now."

As if to demonstrate, Irene turns and noses Sean in the crotch. He dodges back before she can do any real damage.

"Whoa, hey," he says. "We're not even on a first name basis yet."

"Sorry about that," I tell him. "You're lucky she lost her antlers last week. Otherwise, you might have lost a testicle."

Awesome, Amber. Say "testicle" to a man you've just met.

Sean seems unfazed. He reaches out to scratch Vixen's forehead, his long fingers skimming the stubs where her antlers used to be.

"She looks kind of like a cow without the antlers. Why'd she lose them?"

"It happens every year," I assure him. "Males and females both, though the boys usually lose them a little earlier in the season than the girls do."

"Does it hurt?"

"Probably a little. Maybe like losing a tooth as a kid?"

"Hi, sweetheart." He's rubbing her nose now, and Irene leans into him like the brazen hussy she is. He strokes his hands down both sides of her neck, and it might be the first time I've felt jealous of a reindeer.

"There's usually a gap between when they lose the first antler and the second," I prattle on like a deranged science teacher. "So they spend a few days walking around lopsided."

"That sounds awkward." Irene is practically purring now, pressing her whole body against Sean's.

"Floozy," I whisper, earning a laugh from Sean.

"She has cool looking eyes."

"See how they're all white around here? That's another sign she's in heat. I mean, if it weren't already obvious from how she's practically humping you."

I need to stop talking about reindeer sex. Or sex of any kind. Wasn't I the one who said we needed to keep things professional?

"Anyway, this is the space," I tell him. "We can hold weddings outside in the pasture when it's warm, and there's the chapel, of course."

"A chapel?" Sean's eyebrows lift. "You have a chapel on the property?"

I nod, a little pleased by how impressed he sounds. "My great-grandparents built it. They held church services back in the day. It's mostly been sitting empty for the last hundred years or so."

"I'd love to see it," he says. "I'm kind of a history buff."

"Come on. We still have some daylight left."

I lead the way to the other end of the barn and push through the door. The path is darker out here, and the shadowy shapes of reindeer amble along the fence line like creepy statues with branches on their heads.

"That's Harold and Tammy over there," I tell him.

"Do they have stage names?"

"Donner and Dasher. Tammy's knocked up right now."

"Is Harold the father?"

I laugh and shake my head. "I hope not. He's castrated. Artificial insemination is safer for the herd."

"Doesn't sound quite as enjoyable," Sean muses, shooting me a look that might be flirty or might not. I can't tell.

"It is if you're a female," I tell him. "We had to stop breeding after Harold picked Sydney up in his antlers and held her like that for an hour."

Sean shoots me a grimace. "Sounds like a guy who needs to refine his technique."

"Or lose it entirely. That's why he got the snip."

I wonder if normal girls spend this much time talking with attractive men about animal sex and genitals. Then I remind myself this is a business relationship, not a date. Maybe awkward is okay.

"Here we are." I unlock the chapel door and push it open, flicking the lights to illuminate the sanctuary.

Sean moves behind me, and I step aside so he can get the full view. Twelve rows of antique pews line each side of the room, with a narrow aisle between them. The woodwork gleams from the fresh coat of varnish, and the air swirls with cinnamon from the potpourri sachets I tucked under each seat. Pinkish light streams through the skylights as the sun snuggles down behind the mountains for the evening.

"Oh my God," Seth breathes. "This is unbelievable. You own this?"

"Yep." My chest bubbles with pride, but I keep myself from grinning too big. "It's how we came up with the idea for doing weddings. It seemed like a shame to have this beautiful building just standing empty."

"Is this woodwork original?" He runs a hand along the back row of pews, and I nod.

"Most of it. Our dad helped us rebuild that area up there by the pulpit. It got wrecked in a windstorm a few years back."

"Those windows look new." He gestures to a gleaming bank of glass that offers a view of the snow-capped Cascades draped in orangey-pink sunset.

"We put those in last year. There used to be this old stained-glass piece, but it had a really weird crack that made it look like Jesus was peeing on the disciples."

"I can see why that wouldn't be the ideal backdrop for a wedding."

I skim a hand over the windowsill, sending a puff of dust into a sunbeam. "When we were little, Jade told me the dust motes were fairies."

I don't know why I just told him that, but he looks at me like he's noticing something new about me. Something he likes.

"Gotta love sisters," he says. "Mine convinced me to eat a mud pie once."

"Let's hope you've refined your palate since then."

Sean grins and turns toward the window. A sunbeam catches his eyes, and I lose my breath.

Those eyes. My God.

A memory hits me of the stained-glass window before we took it out. There was a panel of forest green in the bottom corner, and when the light hit it at sunrise, it bloomed with an otherworldly green glow.

Sean's eyes are like that.

His gaze swings back to mine, and I have to force myself to breathe again. "I can't imagine having this kind of family history," he says.

"Your dad's property—er, your property, I guess—there's some cool historical stuff there, right?"

He shrugs. "An old barn we did our best to preserve. The pond has been there forever."

A faint smile tugs the corners of his mouth, and I remember his skinny-dipping story. I had no idea he witnessed that, and I find myself blushing unexpectedly.

"There's a cave," Sean says, the shape of his smile shifting to something more nostalgic. "On the north side of our property, under that big rock outcropping."

"The one that looks like a giant dick." I hear my own words in my head and grimace. "It's probably rude to point out a big penis pillar on your neighbor's property."

Sean laughs. "Only if the neighbor is unaware of it. Bree used to call it Boner Rock. She never knew the cave was there until I showed it to her last week."

"Was it your hideout as a kid?"

"Sort of." He touches a hand to the back of a pew. "I used to hang out in there playing with these old pots and pans I found, pretending to be a TV chef."

"Wow." I picture Sean as a freckle-faced boy making dirt soup for imaginary dinner guests. "Did you always want to be a chef?"

He gets an odd look on his face and glances away. "I suppose so."

I'm not sure how to read his expression, or if he wants me to just drop it. He's running a hand over the pulpit, but seems a little lost in thought.

"It must be cool to have this kind of family history," he says. "I never knew my great-grandparents. The ones who used to own property out here."

"You said they were your mom's grandparents?"

"Yeah, but my mother hasn't set foot out here since I was a baby." He shrugs. "She referred to the property as 'Cort's little playground.' Didn't even fight him for it in the divorce."

"Oh." I'm not sure what to say to that. "I hope she did okay in the settlement. Some women get screwed."

His laugh is sharp and a little hollow. "Oh, she did just fine. Got the ski house in Aspen and the condo overlooking Central Park that used to belong to Bree's mother, but my dad did something shady with the title, and my mother's lawyer pounced. Oh, she also got the villa in Milan and—"

"Oh, wow." I bite back a snarky comment about seeing how the other half lives. "So she's doing okay."

He doesn't respond to that. Just turns and studies a thick maple beam next to the side door. He steps closer and peers at the letters carved there. "JK + SP forever." He turns back to me. "This looks old."

"My grandpa carved it when he was thirteen." I step closer

and trace a finger over the familiar carving. "He fell in love with a girl who lived two farms over."

Sean studies the letters with a look that's almost reverent. "I love that you left it here."

"They were married fifty-three years before he died. It seemed like good luck."

He turns again, and the sun catches his eyes just so. Dust motes dance in front of his face, and I hold my breath to squelch the urge to reach for him. He waves a hand through the sunbeam, scattering the twinkly particles. "Looks like your fairies are still here."

"Looks like it." My voice comes out breathy, and I hope he can't read my mind. That he can't tell how much his closeness is affecting me.

"For me, it was mermaids," he says. "My father told me they lived in the pond. I used to stand out on the back deck watching for them at night."

There's that swell of embarrassment again, pinching the center of my chest—the realization that I had an audience that night I got busted for skinny-dipping. I'm determined not to let it get to me. "So that's why you were spying on me that night? You were mermaid hunting?"

He grins and tilts his head toward me. "You did seem like some kind of mythical creature," he says. "I always wondered what you were really like. In real life, not in mermaid fantasies."

Interesting. "And now that you've met me?"

He looks at me a long time with such intensity my throat gets tight. "You're different than I expected."

"How do you mean?"

He must read the confused look on my face. "I didn't mean that in a bad way," he says quickly. "You're more...*real*. Complex."

"Complex." I'm not sure if that's a bad thing or a good thing, but the way he's looking at me suggests the latter. His eyes lock with mine, and my heartbeat does a funny little kick-step.

There's a flicker of heat in his eyes, and I wonder if I'm not the only one whose thoughts keep straying to kissing. We stand there staring at each other in the pinkish light, breathing in dust and cinnamon and something more carnal than sunbeams.

A soft buzz fills the silence, and it takes me a second to realize it's a phone. My butt isn't vibrating, so it must be Sean's.

"Is someone calling you?"

He pulls out a sleek silver iPhone and frowns. "My mother."

I wait for him to elaborate, but maybe he doesn't need to. The thud of those three syllables says a lot.

"Do you need to answer?" I ask.

He shakes his head and stuffs the phone back in his pocket. "No. Not right now." He clears his throat. "Want to go try the food?"

"I'd love to."

We turn and make our way back toward the house, detouring to Sean's car for a cooler and a lidded tray that I carry carefully along the grass-lined path that leads to the wide front porch.

"What's in here?" I ask, hoping he didn't just hear my stomach growl.

"You're holding smoked salmon bruschetta with capers and chive cheese spread," he says. "And I've got ricotta butternut squash soup shooters with crème fraiche and toasted hazelnuts, plus some Caesar salad in mini parmesan cups, along with a phyllo tart with melted brie, caramelized onion, and roasted pear. All sourced from around Oregon, by the way."

"Oh my God, that sounds incredible." My stomach growls again. "That's exactly what the wedding couples have been asking for."

"I aim to please."

I shoulder the front door open and lead Sean up the stairs to the kitchen. As I set my platter on the concrete countertop, Sean starts unpacking the cooler. "I didn't do the full presentation thing with fancy plates and utensils," he says. "I wanted to let the food speak for itself this time."

"Mmm, right now it's saying 'eat me!'"

Sean doesn't look up, but a funny look crosses his face. Did I seriously just say "eat me" to a hot guy in my kitchen?

Face flaming, I turn and busy myself with getting plates and napkins and silverware out of the cupboards. I'm about to suggest we move to the dining room when he thrusts something at me.

"Here, try this." He holds a tiny little cup fashioned out of crisp parmesan and filled with the littlest Caesar salad I've ever seen in my life. I take it from him and pop it in my mouth. My taste buds flood with flavor and texture and so much yummy goodness I moan.

"God, that's amazing."

"Those are always really popular at weddings," he says. "And they pair beautifully with the soup shooters."

He hands me a tiny paper cup that's still steaming, and I take a slow sip. Then a bigger one. Holy wow. "This is incredible. Jade would love this." I down the rest of it in one sip and set the cup on the counter.

Sean smiles, then makes an odd little gesture. "You've got parmesan on your upper lip."

Great. Super sexy.

"Where?" I wipe at my mouth, determined to get it, but Sean shakes his head.

"No, not there."

"Where?" I swipe at my face like a whisker-cleaning hamster, but I can tell from his expression I'm failing. "Show me."

He seems to hesitate, then reaches for me. For a second, I think he just plans to point. That's why his touch sends a white-hot electric arc from my lip to my toes. I suck in a breath as his thumb skims the corner of my mouth.

"There," he murmurs, but doesn't draw his hand back.

We stand there looking into each other's eyes, neither of us blinking. My heart pounds in my ears, and I know he's going to kiss me. Or maybe I'm going to kiss him. I'm honestly not sure who starts it. Only that we move toward each other like two balloons pulled by static.

His lips touch mine, and his palm curves to cup my face. The kiss is soft at first, tinged with nutmeg and sweetness. It quickly turns more urgent, and I stretch up on tiptoe to deepen it. He groans as the tip of my tongue grazes his, and he pulls me against him with one hand on my backside.

He slides his fingers into my hair, and I press my body against the length of him. We're still kissing, but it's more than that now. Our hands are greedy and eager, clawing at fabric, skimming hemlines, grasping for more.

"Amber," he murmurs against my neck as he dots soft kisses in the space below my ear. "You taste so good."

"Don't stop." I clutch at his hair, eager for him to keep going, to kiss his way down my throat, between my breasts.

Good Lord, this guy can kiss. The perfect balance of soft and rough, gentle and eager. I let my hands explore his back, amazed at how muscular he is. The tree-felling, gourmet-meal-cooking thing is working for him. His lips travel over my collarbone, and I will him to keep going. To press me back against the counter and—

A blast of music vibrates from Sean's back pocket, and it takes me a second to register what it is. I pull back and stare at his butt.

"Is your phone playing 'Sisters are Doin' it for Themselves?'"

Sean steps back and fumbles the phone from his back pocket like it's on fire. "I'm sorry, I thought I'd turned that off." He hits something to make it stop ringing, then frowns down at the screen. "Jesus, Bree—eight text messages?"

"Your sister," I say, relieved it's not a girlfriend he failed to mention. "Do you need to respond?"

His gaze sweeps over the screen, and I watch as the color

drains from his face. When he looks up, there's something unreadable in his expression. "I—uh—can I call her back real quick?"

"Of course," I say, waving him toward the stairs. "There's an office on the first floor if you want some privacy."

"Thanks."

He's already dialing the phone as he walks away, and I dig my nails into my palms and say a silent prayer everyone is okay. It's only been a year since he lost his father, so the last thing he needs is another family tragedy.

I busy myself unpacking the rest of the food, resisting the urge to eavesdrop. It's none of my business, and clearly there's some kind of urgent situation. I've only met his sister a few times, but Bree doesn't seem like the kind of woman to cause unnecessary hysterics.

I turn when I hear footsteps on the landing. Sean moves slowly up the stairs, his jaw set in a rigid mask. There's a smudge of pink lip gloss at the edge of his mouth, and I flush at the memory of putting it there.

When his eyes meet mine, my breath stalls in an awkward little hiccup.

"I'm so sorry," he says. "I have to go."

I grip the edge of the counter. "Is everything okay?"

Of course everything's not okay. The guy is white as a ghost, but he nods.

"Yeah. No one's hurt or anything," he says. "I just—there's a situation with my mother."

Yikes. "I hope she's all right. Here, let me get the food packed up."

"No, you keep it." He's already shrugging into his coat. "I'll stop by some other time to grab the cooler."

I stop gathering food and stand with my hands useless at my sides. "Sure, no problem. Or I could bring it by later if that's easier for you."

"No. No, that's okay. I—I don't know how long I'll be tied up with—with this situation." His words are rushed, and he's shaking his head like he wants to say more. "I'll give you a call." He gives me a smile that seems forced, but it's a good effort. "Don't worry, everything's fine."

If that's true, Sean's idea of *fine* is way different from mine.

But I smile anyway, wishing there was something I could do. Some way to make it better, whatever "it" might be.

"Let me know if I can help," I tell him.

"Thanks. I will." He seems to hesitate a moment, then takes a step closer. "Hey." He closes the distance between us and reaches up to cup a palm over my cheek. Just like that, every nerve in my body starts humming again.

"Thank you," he murmurs, his gaze holding mine.

"For what?"

His lips brush mine in a kiss that's sweet and lingering. A kiss I'll be feeling for days. It's soft and gentle so dizzying that I forget I've asked a question until he draws back.

"For this," he says.

Then he steps back and gives me a funny little wistful smile. I flatten my palms on the counter, fighting the urge to reach for him again.

Sean takes another step back and shoves his hands in his coat pockets. "I'll call you," he says. "Thanks for understanding."

"No problem."

And with that, he hurries away, leaving me with a thousand questions and the tingling memory of his lips on mine.

CHAPTER 4

SEAN

I step into the dim light of my restaurant foyer feeling like a teenager arriving for an awkward first date. The sun is almost gone, but the overhead lights haven't kicked on yet, giving the dining room an otherworldly glow.

There she is.

Melody Bannon Bracelyn Buchanan, better known as Chef Melody on the Food Network's hit show *Harmonious Kitchen.*

She's a world expert on food and wine pairings, and also marrying men with like-sounding surnames.

Her back is to me as she gazes out over the backlit peaks of the Cascade Mountains, which gives me a chance to study her. She's wearing sea green cashmere and diamond hoops the size of silver dollars. Her hair is styled in a complicated updo that'll be un*done* by the first big gust of Central Oregon wind. Not that she spends much time outdoors.

I clear my throat. "Mother."

She turns with a casualness I can tell is feigned. Like it's the most normal thing in the world for her to show up here in Oregon at the ranch she hasn't set foot on since I wore diapers.

I survey her eyes for signs of trouble. She's good at hiding it.

All I can make out is cool, glassy blue, and a tiredness I don't think was there the last time I saw her.

"Darling." She gives me a smile that seems genuine. Slowly, with practiced elegance, she gets to her feet and glides toward me like she's walking the runway at Fashion Week. "You're looking marvelous, sweetheart. It's wonderful to see you."

She takes both my hands in hers and stretches up to give her standard-issue air kisses that land somewhere in the vicinity of my ears. I consider hugging her just to see how she'd react, but that's not how it is with us. Melody Bannon Bracelyn Buchanan doesn't hug.

"What brings you all the way to Oregon?" I'm trying hard to sound cheerful and casual, but the words land with a dull thump.

If my mother notices, she doesn't react.

"I wanted to surprise you, darling," she says. "You've been working so hard, and I wanted to admire all the progress you've made."

"I see." I don't see, actually, but odds are slim she'll tell me more than that. Not until she's good and ready.

"Besides, the show is on hiatus to gear up for ratings sweeps. You know how it is."

"Sure," I say, even though I don't. It's not like my mother keeps me in the loop with the details of her hit TV show. She used to mail me autographed photos when I was at boarding school, and I'd tack them on my corkboard above my desk.

My classmates had a heyday with that one.

"Can I get you something?" I ask, settling for my usual fall-back. "Perrier, maybe a soda? I got this new elderflower syrup from Italy, and I've been experimenting with this great mocktail using fresh mint and—"

"Veuve Clicquot, please," she says, her pronunciation immaculate as she waves toward the bar. "I saw you have some in the chiller."

I try not to let her see me wince. It's not like I'm surprised my mother has been prowling through my coolers, and I'm sure as hell not surprised she thinks nothing of popping open a hundred-dollar bottle of champagne.

For a second, I think about arguing. Telling her money's been tight as we gear up to open the resort.

But hell, it's not every day that my mother shows up in Oregon to see me. Maybe I don't need to be a dick about the champagne.

"Coming right up," I say tightly as I retreat toward the kitchen.

There's some butternut squash soup and a few parmesan cups left from the food I made for Amber, so I throw together a bit more Caesar salad and a little of the onion tart. I'm trying not to think about Amber, but how can I not?

I can still feel her lips full and soft and lush against mine. Her hair smelled like sunshine and honeysuckle and slid silky between my fingers. My ears echo with that soft whimpering sound she made as she pressed her body against me.

How the hell did that happen?

And how can I make it happen again?

Focus, I order myself as I pile the food onto one of the hand-carved cheeseboards, already anticipating a lecture from my mother on the germ-harboring properties of wood. Who the hell cares what she thinks?

You do. You always did.

I cram the champagne bottle in an ice-filled bucket and tuck it in the crook of my arm, balancing the cheese tray and the glasses and a whole lot of emotional baggage as I make my way back out to the dining area.

"Here we go." I push through the doors and return to the table with as much enthusiasm as I can muster. I set down the cheese board and while my mother surveys it, I wrestle with the champagne. The cork pops like a gun blast, but my mother doesn't flinch.

"Thank you, dear." She accepts the champagne flute and takes a dainty sip, her fingers blinking with diamonds that sparkle like bubbles in the glass. "Very nice. Not quite as good as the Armand de Brignac I had in France a few weeks ago, but still very elegant."

Why are you really here?

I want to yell it, to scream it, but I keep my face fixed in a mask of blank neutrality. I focus on pouring my own glass of champagne, watching the bubbles fizz like nervous bumblebees.

"A toast." I lift my glass, determined to make the best of things. "To reunions."

"To reunions." She smiles and clinks her glass against mine, then takes another drink. "It really is good to see you."

There's an earnestness in her tone that surprises me. Her eyes are wide and filled with something unfamiliar. Remorse? No, that can't be it. It's gone in an instant anyway, leaving me with a familiar bitterness on the back of my tongue. I swallow a mouthful of champagne to wash it down, but it doesn't go away. Neither does the flood of memory clouding my head.

Springtime, third grade, Melody Bannon Bracelyn Buchanan appeared as if by magic in the foyer of Willington Academy. She'd avoided all the formal visitation dates at my boarding school up to that point, insisting she was too busy with her filming schedule.

But there she was that day, materializing in the lobby as though conjured by the sheer force of my homesickness.

"Darling!" she called, throwing her arms open wide. That's all it took. All it ever took for me to go rushing toward her like an affection-starved cat. We stood there hugging in the foyer while my classmates spilled around us like water. I remember feeling warm all over, like a rock in the sun, and I held on to my mother like my life depended on it.

It's one of the few hugs I remember. One of the last, too.

I take another sip of champagne to pull myself back to the present. "Do you have a hotel room in town?"

She tips her head to the side, studying me like a zebra that wandered into her parlor. "Actually, I was hoping to stay here."

"Here?"

"It's a resort, isn't it?"

"Right, but we're not open yet." I wave in the general direction of the upstairs lodge suites still awaiting commodities like beds and plush robes. "We can't legally allow anyone to stay on the premises. Not until our permits are approved."

My mother looks at me, assessing, but saying nothing. I hesitate, not liking the taste of the words I'm about to utter. I know I'm going to regret this.

"My cabin has two master suites," I say slowly. "If you'd like, I could let you stay in—"

"I'd love to." She swirls the liquid in her glass, making the bubbles shimmer. "Oh, this will be so fun. Just like when you were little."

Something in my gut clenches up like a rubber band ball, but I nod anyway. "The guest suite has those European linens you always liked. Bree bought sets for the whole resort."

"Wonderful, darling. What's the Wi-Fi password here? I'm expecting an important email from my manager."

I rattle it off, then set down my champagne flute at the edge of the table while she types in the password. She finishes tapping the screen and sets down her phone, then reaches for my hand. I jerk at the unexpected touch.

"It really is wonderful to see you," she says. "You look tired."

Her eyes fill with concern that seems totally fucking genuine, and it socks me right in the gut. Hard, like someone punched me. Jesus. I hate that it takes so little for me to curl up like a dog that's been waiting for his owner to come home.

Just like that, I'm a goddamn third grader again.

My mother pulls her hand back and reaches across the table

to pluck the champagne bottle from the chiller. "Tell me more about what you're doing here," she says as she refills her glass. "It looks like you've been working really hard."

I stare at her for a second, surprised by the turn in conversation. She hasn't shown much interest in the ranch so far, not even when she learned dear old dad willed us the place.

"Well," I say, not sure where to start. "We're still a few months from opening. That's assuming we get all the permits and approvals in time."

"And how many rooms and amenities and all that?" She beams and sips her champagne. "Seriously, tell me everything, darling. I'm wildly curious."

I scrub a hand through my hair, wishing Bree were here to give her marketing spiel. She's making herself scarce, never a big fan of my mother, who once slapped Bree's mom for suggesting wife number four—Mark's mother—might actually stick.

She didn't, but that's beside the point.

"Let's see," I say. "The resort is about a thousand acres, and we have lodging options that run from deluxe ranch house suites in the main lodge, to luxury cabins that range from two-bedroom units to massive lodge houses meant for large parties."

"Of course, for family vacations and such." My mother smiles. "Remember that time we all went to Montenegro?"

I'm rattled by the memory, and it takes me a second to think of a response. "I was six?"

"Seven, actually. It was right before your father left me for that whore but after the Kentucky Derby."

I nod, accustomed to how the timeline of her life flows around my father's infidelities. "Right. Um, it was nice."

"It was nice, wasn't it? Such wonderful memories." She pats my hand again, and I can't help wondering why she's trying so hard. "So there's a spa and golf courses and an event center?"

"That's right." I run my thumb through a ring of moisture at the base of my champagne flute. "Did Bree give you a tour already?"

"No, I've been looking at your website. So much great information."

I nod and pick at a soup shooter. "That's Bree's doing. The photography is stunning."

"Yes, I particularly like the one of Boner Rock at sunset."

"What?" I nearly knock my champagne flute into my lap as I stare at my mother. "Did you say Boner Rock?"

My mother laughs and sips her champagne. "Relax, darling. Don't think I don't know that's what everyone calls it."

"I thought that was just Bree's term."

"There's a lot more history here than you think."

No shit.

There's a sting in the center of my chest that's halfway between joy and pain. It's always been like this, every moment I can remember with my mother. This aching mix of anger and longing, sadness, and shame.

Maybe this time will be different.

I clear my throat, not sure my voice still works. "I've missed you."

My mother looks up and smiles. Her expression is more relaxed now, and I dart a glance at the champagne bottle, wondering if that's the reason.

"I've missed you, too." She smiles and reaches for one of my mini phyllo tarts with melted brie, caramelized onion, and roasted pear. I wonder if she'll recognize the recipe as a riff of something she made on her show.

"So you'll be running your own restaurant here," she says. "It's very nice."

"Thanks." I twirl my champagne glass on the tabletop. "We're already booking dinner reservations a couple years out for some of the holidays."

"Of course you are," my mother says, lifting her champagne

flute. "It's not every day some backwater Oregon town gets a restaurant owned by a Michelin-starred chef."

The pride in her voice makes my chest swell, but it also makes my gut clench. It's time to stop beating around the bush.

"Mother?"

"Yes, darling?"

"Why are you really here?"

Her smile wavers just a little, but she recovers fast, the corners of her mouth tugging up like her lips are being pulled by wires. "I can't come see my only child for the pleasure of his company?"

"Sure you can." I clear my throat. "But you haven't. Not when I was living in Austin or LA or even when I was in Paris at Le Cordon Bleu."

"Maybe I decided it's time for us to be closer."

"Maybe." I eye her, certain there's more to the story. Younger me would drop his gaze, but I hold firm.

"There is one teeny-tiny issue," she says.

My fingers tighten around the stem of the champagne flute, but I refuse to let her see me react. "Okay."

"It's something my lawyer brought up last week when we were doing my financial review. I'm sure it's nothing."

"Let's hear it."

She waves a dismissive hand, champagne sloshing in her glass. "There's apparently some question over whether your father followed the law when he set up this property. When he acquired all the different parcels that make up the total acreage."

"What, you mean your grandparents' place?"

"Yes, along with some of the other pieces of land," she says. "You know how he was. Never one to do things by the books."

I take a few breaths, willing myself not to overreact. "What are you saying?"

She hesitates, then sets her champagne flute on the table. "That there's some question about whether my grandparents' land was legally added to the parcel. Something to do with property taxes and title transfers—my lawyer explained it all to me. I'd be happy to give you his card."

There's a buzzing in my head, and I watch her grab the bottle again and fill her glass to the brim. The bubbles fizz like the pit of my stomach.

"I don't understand," I say slowly.

"I don't, either, darling," she says. "But bottom line, it's possible your father didn't have the legal right to will this property to anyone."

Something in my brain buzzes as I watch my mother drain half her glass in one sip. "I don't—"

"Now don't you worry," she says, patting my arm. "We'll get this cleared up in no time. I'm sure it's just a minor technicality. But in the meantime, I'd love to stay with you until things are straightened out."

I swallow hard and watch her tip the empty champagne bottle into her glass, determined to get the last few drops. I feel queasy, but the feeling isn't unfamiliar.

"I'm going to need to tell the others," I say. "Bree and Mark and James and—"

"Let's not talk about this now, shall we?" She swirls the last of the champagne in her glass. "I'm too excited about catching up with you."

"Sure." I swallow back the unspoken words, their familiar shape burning all the way down my throat.

* * *

IT TAKES LESS than twenty-four hours for three of my siblings to corner me. At least they have the good sense to do it in the restaurant.

"Is your mother settled in at your place?" Bree asks, folding her hands on the table. She's fixing me with a look that says she'd

49

doesn't particularly care about the answer and wishes we could fast forward through the niceties and get to the real conversation.

My brother, Mark, doesn't bother. "What the actual fuck?"

He slings his six-foot-five frame into one of our hand-carved dining room chairs, straddling it like he's in a dive bar. He rubs a hand over his lumberjack beard and stares at me. "Seriously, dude, what the fuck is up with your mom?"

Bree drops her folded hands to her lap and glares at him. "We were going to be tactful about this, remember?"

Mark grunts but says nothing.

Our oldest brother, James, clears his throat. He's not bothering to sit down. A recovering attorney, he looks like someone getting ready to deliver closing arguments in a criminal trial.

"Look, we're concerned, that's all." James rests his hands on the back of a chair and stares me down. "You have to admit, your mother has a reputation for shady real estate deals."

Bree's chin lifts a fraction of an inch, while Mark mutters a creative string of profanity. I'm itching to run to the kitchen and throw together a six-course meal that will make us forget about this conversation and our mothers and our collective messed up childhoods. Open communication is not my specialty, but salt-baked leg of lamb is. Or salmon poached in white wine. Or—really, anything but this conversation.

"I get it, I do." I look at Bree. "I know my mother wasn't very gracious about evicting your mom from the New York penthouse after the settlement. And James, you have every right to be pissed about the way things went down with the Aspen property."

Mark folds his arms over his chest. "It's not about that," he says. "My mom was broke as shit with nothing for your mom to steal. I still don't trust her any farther than I could throw her."

My brother's arms are the size of tree trunks, and I don't doubt he could throw my mom pretty far. I also don't doubt he's considered it.

None of my father's divorces were friendly.

I turn to James, eager for his rational approach to things. "You've been in touch with her lawyer?"

He gives a tight nod. "She's not wrong. There's definitely something odd about the titles on some of the parcels that got added together to form this ranch."

"Odd like 'ha ha,' or odd like, 'let's lawyer up?'" Bree asks.

"Somewhere between those two," James says carefully. "I've got our lawyers looking into it."

I take a deep breath and run my hands down the thighs of my jeans. "Look, I don't blame you guys for not trusting my mother."

Bree's expression softens, and she looks at me for a few minutes before speaking. "It's nothing personal. We just—" she hesitates, then glances at the others before speaking. "You've always had a blind spot when it comes to her."

"We all do," James says. "With our own mothers, that is."

Mark gives a grunt of acknowledgement but doesn't add anything. He once saved his mom from a house fire, so he doesn't need to say a damn thing.

Bree sighs. "Having a serial philanderer for a father probably gave us all big gobs of trust issues."

"True enough," James says. "And it goes without saying that we've all heard unflattering stories about each other's mothers."

"That's for damn sure," Mark mutters.

I feel myself stiffen but try not to let them see it. How much do they know?

For that matter, how much do I know?

I clear my throat and look to James. "I can appreciate your concern," I say. "And I'm all for looking into things with the attorneys. But for right now, can we take it at face value that she's just here to visit?"

Three pairs of eyes flash with skepticism. Mark and James are the first to look away, but Bree watches me until I feel myself shifting in my chair. "Aren't you at least a tiny bit suspicious?" she asks. "About why she's here and what she has up her sleeve."

"Of course," I say.

More than you know.

"Look, our goddamn livelihood is on the line," Mark says. "Dad left this shithole to us, and we've turned it into something pretty fucking amazing."

"I'll be sure to use that line in our marketing materials," Bree says dryly. "Seriously, though—let's be careful."

"Agreed," James says, and we all nod. I say a silent prayer this conversation is almost over.

I feel Mark's eyes on me, and I turn to see my brother staring. He's looking at me like he can see straight through my skull, and I wonder what he'd say if he could read my mind.

"Keep your fucking eyes open," he mutters, then slugs me in the shoulder. "We love you, asshole. And we don't want anything bad to happen to you."

"Or to the rest of us," James says. "We're in this together."

"Like the motherfucking Brady Bunch," Bree says. "With adultery and backstabbing."

"There's something for the brochures," Mark grumbles.

I survey my siblings, wishing I could say more. Wishing I *knew* more. Wishing there were something I could do to set their minds at ease.

Wishing, for the thousandth time, I could do something about my mother.

CHAPTER 5

AMBER

I'm ten minutes into my meeting with another bride-to-be when I notice the smell. Sort of a funky, sweet-and-sour odor with strange notes of lilac.

"You promise you don't think I'm a psycho?" Beth Cahill's expression is so earnest that I stop sniffing and reach across the table to squeeze her hand.

"You're not a psycho," I assure her, though I'm not totally convinced. "I think it's natural to reflect on past relationships as a way of growing and moving forward."

The bride-to-be stares down at her engagement ring with a sheepish expression. "I'm not sure that's why I asked you to tell me about Greg's wedding," she says softly. "But it's sweet of you to say so."

I do another discreet inhale, noticing the scent again. At first I thought it was Beth, but it seems like it's on my side of the desk. Maybe I stepped in something?

"Weddings bring up a lot of funny emotions in people," I offer, my brain only half on the conversation.

"That's true," Beth says. "I know our wedding's not until June and Greg's is next week, but that's still pretty close together," she continues. "You're sure you don't mind doing some investigating?"

Spying is what she means, but I refrain from saying so. I also refrain from admitting that I'm starting to think the funky smell might be *me*. Did I forget deodorant?

"I was planning to be at Greg's wedding anyway, so it's really no big deal," I tell her.

"Just a few notes on flowers and dresses and centerpieces and things like that," Beth continues, oblivious to the odd odor. Am I imagining it?

I clear my throat to focus and ask the question I probably should have asked at the start of this conversation. "You're not still in love with him, are you?"

I wouldn't be this blunt with anyone who hadn't shared my 64-pack of Crayolas in second grade. Beth shakes her head so violently a bobby pin falls out of her hair.

"No! Absolutely not." She bites her lip. "It's just—have you ever felt like you had something to prove after getting out of a relationship that was all wrong?"

"Relation*ships*," I murmur, emphasis on the plural. "Yes."

All the damn time.

Beth gives a shaky smile. "I knew you'd get it. And I promise I'm not looking for top secret info. Just stuff about decorations and the ceremony so I can be sure I don't duplicate anything."

"I've got you," I assure her. I glance down, wondering if there's something on my shoe. It doesn't smell like reindeer droppings, and there's no discreet way to check. "I'm usually pretty observant at weddings anyway, so I'll pay extra attention for you."

"Thanks, Amber. I knew I could count on you." There's that slightly embarrassed look again, but Beth holds my gaze this time. "I used to be crazy jealous of you."

"Of me?" I frown at her, weird smells forgotten for the moment.

She gives a self-deprecating little shrug. "You were always so damn perfect. Flawless Amber, captain of the soccer team, student body president, nicest person anyone could hope to meet." She winces and shakes her head. "I don't mean that as a bad thing. I don't know why that came out sounding snarky."

"It's okay," I say, wondering if she'd think I'm Miss Perfect if she knew I'm pretty sure I'm wearing a funky-smelling bra. When's the last time I washed it? I clear my throat. "It's been a long time—um—since high school."

Beth laughs, oblivious to my distress. Not just from the bra-stink, but from this line of conversation. "All the girls wanted to be you," she says, "and all the boys wanted to scr—"

"So I'll just email you those quotes from the DJ," I interrupt, tapping my pen on the desk. "And we'll go from there on deciding how to handle your music."

Beth gives me an apologetic smile and gets to her feet. I follow suit, and she pulls me into a Chanel-scented hug. I grimace, hoping like hell she doesn't inhale too deeply. "Thanks, Amber. You really are the best."

"You, too."

I watch her exit my office in the corner of the barn and make her way to the side door and out into the crisp spring afternoon. The second the barn door closes, I yank my sweater off one shoulder and sniff my bra strap.

Nothing. It just smells like the lilac body lotion I've been wearing lately.

But I know I smell something, and I'm pretty sure I'm on the right track. I pull both arms inside my shirt sleeves and contort them behind me to unhook my bra. Mission accomplished, I snake the offending garment through the left sleeve of my sweater and pull it out at the wrist like a deranged magician.

I hold up the bra for inspection, but it looks fine. Lavender and lacy, it's one of my nicest pieces of lingerie. But when did I last wash it?

I hold it to my nose and have just started to inhale when the barn door flies open.

"Amber, hey—oh." Sean freezes halfway to my office, blinking against the dim light of the barn. And at the sight of me smelling my bra.

Slowly, I lower my hands to the desk and lay the lacy scrap there like a dead pet. "Sean."

He looks at me, then at the bra, then back to my face, detouring only a little at my unsupported assets hidden beneath magenta cashmere. "I—uh—" He steps forward, hesitating at the door of my office. "Your sister said you were out here. I came by to grab my coolers?"

A quicker-thinking woman might shove the bra in a desk drawer or try to pass it of as a hanky.

I've never been that quick.

"So—I—right." I take a deep breath and gesture toward the lavender lace laid out on my desk with the cups pointing jauntily at the ceiling. "I suppose you're wondering why I'm smelling my bra."

"The thought did occur to me." He leans against the doorframe, and I can tell he's trying not to smile.

I drop into my desk chair with a little more bounce than expected. Sean's eyes flicker, but he keeps them on my face.

"Right, see, there are certain things no one really tells you when you're a girl."

He hesitates, then settles into Beth's vacated seat. "Okay."

"Like everyone knows you wash your panties every day, right?"

"One can assume." He's having a harder time holding back laughter, I can tell.

"But no one ever sits you down and says, 'here's how often you should wash your bras.' Like is it once a week? Every few days? Monthly? I honestly don't know, and then how do you remember which ones you washed when and whether there's this one random bra in the back of the drawer that got skipped the last time you did delicates, and now you're pretty sure it's been years since the damn thing saw soap and water?"

My voice has risen to the pitch of a crazy person, to say nothing about my actual words. My God, he must think I'm insane.

Slowly, the smile spreads over his face. He folds his hands on the desk, and I'm conscious of the fact that his knuckles are scant inches from my favorite bra. Is it wrong that I'm wishing my boobs were still in it?

"You remember what I said in the chapel?" he asks. "About how you're way different from Ethereal Mermaid Amber I used to imagine?"

I nod, not trusting myself not to say another damn word.

"I like this Amber better," he says. "The quirky one who says stuff other people are probably thinking, but don't actually say? I'm digging that about you."

"Right." I swallow hard and lift my own hands to the desk, lacing my fingers together just a few millimeters from his. "Not a lot of people have met that version of Amber."

"Too bad for them."

We sit there looking at each other for a second. I really want to shove my undergarment off the desk, but I'd just be drawing attention to it. And to the fact that I'm sitting here braless talking to the hottest guy I've met in ages. A guy who groped me in my kitchen just a few days ago.

Stirred by the memory, my nipples rise to attention like soldiers reporting for duty. I fold my arms across my chest, but not before Sean's eyes go molten. He doesn't even pretend not to notice, but he does lift his gaze to mine after a few beats. "Did you—uh—want to put that back on?"

I look down at the bra, wondering what etiquette calls for.

I've never seen this in Miss Manners' column. I'm still not sure if the bra smells funky, in which case, maybe I don't want to put it back on. But I'm not about to sniff it in front of Sean, so maybe I just shove it in the drawer and call it good? Or maybe I'm better with it on, weird smell or not.

"I can turn my back if you want," Sean offers. "Or leave."

"Don't leave." The words come out with more urgency than I intended. I yank open the top desk drawer and shove the bra inside, then slam it shut and bite my lip. "Admit it. Is this the most awkward start to a business relationship ever?"

He smiles. "No. That would be me falling off a ladder and conking my head when the most beautiful girl I've ever seen shows up holding a dead turkey."

"Right." My skin goes hot, and I'm having trouble breathing. "There's that."

His smile turns thoughtful. "If it makes you feel better, guys have stuff like that, too. Things we're just expected to know, but no one ever really tells us."

"Like what?"

He leans back in his chair, politely averting his gaze from my boobs. "Well, take jumper cables. When you're a guy, you're just expected to know how they work."

"Or when you're a farm girl."

"See?" He leans forward again, and I admire the flex of his pecs under the thin T-shirt he's wearing. "It's just one of those things certain people *know*, but then you find yourself in a parking lot at a black tie fundraiser with a dead battery and no idea what to do with the damn cables."

I can't say I relate to most of that, but I do get what he's saying. "I was in college before I realized not everyone has eaten Rocky Mountain Oysters."

"Rocky M—you mean calf testicles?" He grimaces.

"Yep. There's a whole festival for it out here. Happens during castration season."

Sean looks pained, and I wonder how the hell I managed to circle back to the subject of testicles. "My junk just shriveled knowing there's an actual season for castration," he says. "Remind me to stay home that week."

I laugh and do my best not to think about Sean's junk. "The Testie Festie has been going for more than twenty years," I tell him. "It's one of those weird traditions that you grow up thinking of as normal until you realize not every kid in your college classes has eaten love spuds."

"Sounds like a real ball."

I smirk. "Yeah, it can be pretty nuts."

He laughs, and the sound makes my whole body vibrate pleasantly. Since I'm still braless, the vibration does not go unnoticed. My nipples pop to attention again, and I consider removing them with my letter opener.

Sean clears his throat and stands up. "I should probably go."

I stand up, too, careful not to jostle too much. "Don't you need me to get the cooler for you?"

"Your sister already grabbed it," he says. "I just came out to say hi."

I press one palm against the desk and hold his gaze for a moment. "You mean you weren't wanting to talk about what happened the other night?"

Crap. I didn't mean to say that out loud.

But now that I've pointed out the elephant in the room, it seems dumb not to stroke its trunk and offer it a scone. Sean seems frozen, so I walk around the desk and plant myself in front of him. "I didn't mean to let things get out of hand the other night," I tell him. "Not that I didn't enjoy it."

"We're really doing this?" Sean looks pained. "Talking about it, I mean?"

"You were planning to avoid this conversation?"

"Always," he says, his expression a little guilty. "That's kinda my MO."

"Good to know." It is, actually, and I file the information in my brain for future reference.

"Amber."

For a second I think that's it. He's going to say goodbye and walk out without another word. The last thing I want is for a guy to stick around talking about a kiss he regrets.

That's why the next kiss is such a shock. One second Sean's standing there looking like a guy ready to flee the premises. The next second his fingers are laced in my hair, and he's kissing me with a softness that rivals the feel of cashmere against my bare breasts.

When he draws back, he keeps one hand cupped against my cheek. There's something explosive in those dark green eyes, and I feel myself go dizzy.

"I don't regret it," he says. "Not one bit."

I lick my lips, tasting his minty Chapstick. "Neither do I."

He drops his hand and takes a few steps back. "I really should go," he says softly. "I don't want to take advantage of—" he gestures to my chest and steps back again.

"You don't trust yourself?" I'm not trying to sound flirty, but Sean gives a guilty smile and shakes his head.

"Not one damn bit." Another step back. "But I really do have to get home. There's a meeting I'm supposed to be at in ten minutes, and my sister will kill me if I'm not there."

"Duty calls," I say faintly, wishing he didn't have to go. Wishing he'd slide his hands up my sweater and cup my breasts in those palms as he presses me back against the desk and—

"To be continued?"

I'm not positive if it's a question or a statement, but I nod anyway. "Yeah. Too be continued."

Even though we said we wouldn't. Even though we both agreed it's not a good idea.

Why was that again?

"Enjoy your night, Amber."

"You, too."

He smiles and turns away, and I don't even pretend I'm not watching his ass as he heads out the barn door. Every nerve in my body feels electrified, and every part of me craves Sean Bracelyn's touch.

Dammit.

CHAPTER 6

SEAN

I've never had a reason to do a Google image search for "awkward family dinner," but if I did, I'm guessing I'd see a photo of my dining room on Friday night.

Seated at the head is my mother, resplendent in a silk kimono she got while filming in Japan.

Beside her is the daughter of the woman whose husband she stole years ago.

"Please pass the bread," Bree says crisply, offering a tight smile when my mother obliges.

The son of said husband's *next* mistress is hunkered on the other side of the table, looking like a grumpy lumberjack eating off a hundred-and-fifty-dollar Boug Joly Ajouree Chevet plate.

Not that I know a damn thing about dishes, but my mother has announced ten thousand times that this china was a gift from one of her show's sponsors. God knows why she had it delivered here. "Mark, dear," she says. "Please pass the butter."

My younger brother looks like he's seriously considering telling her where she can shove the butter, but he decides to be a gentleman.

"Thank you," my mother says. "It's a shame James couldn't make it."

Mark stabs a grape tomato in his salad with such force it spits seeds across the table. "Damn shame," he agrees as he and Bree exchange a look.

I know for a fact James is off researching property titles and real estate law and God knows what else in a quest to get to the bottom of whether my mother could have a claim on this property. The rest of us are doing our damnedest to act like a normal family.

"Darling, may I please have a refill?" my mother lifts her empty wineglass, and I do some quick mental math to determine how much Chenin Blanc we've gone through already. This cheerful family meal is requiring a lot more alcohol than I anticipated.

"So, Breann," my mother says as she hoists her replenished wineglass. "What is it you do here again?"

"I'm the Vice President of Marketing and Events," Bree says, ripping a hunk of sourdough with both hands. "And Mark is the Vice President of Facilities Management."

"Can't we just say handyman?" Mark mutters as he swipes breadcrumbs from his beard with a cloth napkin. "These goddamn fancy titles give me a headache."

Bree ignores him and slathers her bread with a generous slab of butter. "James is Vice President of Operations, and Jonathon—"

"Good Lord, how many of you are there?" My mother laughs at her own joke, but no one laughs with her. It's no secret our father had a host of impressively fertile wives and mistresses, but we don't usually talk about it over dinner. Or anytime, really.

Bree finishes chewing her bread and takes a sip of her wine. She looks at me a moment, then turns back to my mother. "Our job titles and positions are irrelevant," she says. "What matters is that a whole lot of us have invested a great deal of time, talent, and money into launching Ponderosa Luxury Ranch Resort."

Mark nods and picks up his water glass. "And we'd hate for anything to interfere with that."

Jesus, my brother sounds like a mobster. I can't blame him, really. I know this is why my siblings suggested dinner tonight, but part of me is hoping someone chokes on a chicken bone and this whole thing ends quickly.

"It certainly has potential to be a highly profitable business," my mother says, ignoring Bree's grimace. Or maybe she didn't notice it in the first place. She's already drained her wineglass, so it's possible she's missing some nuance. "How many investors are involved?"

"Just us," Bree says, giving her a pointed look. "All of the Bracelyn siblings in one form or another."

I study my mother from across the table, looking for signs that she's ready to crack. This whole damn dinner was a bad idea. Her gaze swings to mine, and she gives a watery smile. "Sean, darling. Tell me about your love life. You know how much I'd adore having grandbabies."

I grip my fork a little tighter as my brain flashes on an image of Amber King. I think of the softness of her lips, the press of her body against mine in the warm solitude of her kitchen. Or the round lushness of her breasts under that pink sweater, the way she arched against me when I kissed her.

There's a surge of something fierce and protective inside me, and I can't say for sure where it's coming from.

"There's no one," I say, reaching for the platter of lemon leek roasted Cornish hens. "More chicken anyone?"

Mark nods and holds out his plate. "Sure, thanks."

I dish him up and set the platter aside as a phone rings from somewhere far away. My mother dabs her mouth with a napkin. "I need to take that," she says, pushing back from her chair and grabbing her wineglass. "Would you excuse me? This could be a little while."

As she hurries from the room, my shoulders start to relax. They hitch up again as I hear the first strains of conversation from the guest room. "Maxwell, darling, please tell me we have a claim."

A door closes at the back of the house, so we can't hear the rest of the conversation. Bree narrows her eyes at me. "Is that her lawyer?"

"Her manager," I say, straining to hear the conversation. I can't make out a damn thing. Why are the walls in this place so thick?

Bree frowns. "Isn't he the guy who put together the deal that screwed my mother over?"

"That was her real estate guy," I say. "Fred someone. Or Floyd. I don't remember; it's been a long time."

Bree doesn't look appeased. Neither does Mark.

"Look, I'm keeping an eye on her, okay?" I glance from my sister to my brother and back again. "Will you trust me on this?"

"We trust you," Mark says. "Not her."

"Understood." I pick up my water glass and drain it, feeling the weight of everyone's trust like a noose around my neck.

I'm fumbling around in my brain for a subject change when Bree saves me. "I had someone come out to look at the cave," she says. "The guy I've been working with from the Warm Springs tribe."

"What did he say?" I ask.

"He didn't find anything that's historically or culturally significant," she says. "There was some old kitchen crap that dates back fifty years or so, but nothing valuable."

"What about the petroglyph stuff?" Mark asks, wiping his beard with a napkin.

"Not petroglyphs, apparently," she says. "Just graffiti or something. Anyway, we're free to do cave tours in there if we want to.

65

Or not." She gives me a pointed look as I shove a leaf of romaine around my plate.

I set down my fork and pick up my own wineglass. "What's that look about?"

"I know it was your special place as a kid," she says slowly. "I don't want to go stepping on your turf."

"It's fine," I assure her, meaning it completely. "This place belongs to all of us. I want what's best for the family."

"Agreed," Bree says, giving me a wary look.

"Damn straight," Mark mutters and lifts his wineglass.

I'M NOT sure what lures me down to the pond a few nights later. The full moon? A need for fresh air? Some weird nostalgia for childhood summers spent looking for mermaids under the stars?

Or maybe it's that I need to get the hell out of the cabin before I murder my mother.

I can still hear her voice in my ears as I trudge down the dirt-caked path, my footsteps thudding in time to her lecture on the proper way to braise pork loin so it pairs perfectly with the Pinot Noir she brought back from yesterday's trip to the Willamette Valley.

The taste of the wine is bitter on the back of my tongue, and I wish I'd thought to brush my teeth before charging out into the crisp night air. Hell, I didn't even grab a flashlight.

Not that I need one. The full moon lights the path, and the night sky is clear and cloudless with bright pinpricks of stars. It's too early in the season for frogs, but the night air swirls with a symphony of other sounds—the hoot of an owl, the far-off yip of coyotes, the burble of the creek tumbling over smooth rocks beside the path.

I breathe in the scent of sagebrush and juniper, remembering the first time I visited here as a boy.

"It smells like heaven," I told my dad.

He sniffed the air and laughed. "Juniper smells like cat piss."

I never saw the connection, but I also never had a cat. Maybe I should remedy that now that I'm living out in the country. A fat, surly tom to catch mice in the woodpile behind my new wood-fired pizza oven. Or maybe a fluffy white Persian who attacks my toes under the covers.

I've almost reached the pond when the back of my neck prickles. Lost in thought about small cats, I've forgotten the big ones. A flash of memory jolts me to Amber's story about the cougar, and I wish like hell I brought a gun. Or owned one. Or had any idea how to fire one.

But it's not danger making my spidey senses tingle. It's something else. Something I can't put my finger on until my frantic gaze lands on the figure standing by the edge of the pond. Bare shoulders catch the moonlight, and dark hair tumbles down the slope of a very naked back.

Oh my God.

My breath catches in my throat. I don't know how long I stand wordless and staring until I finally find my voice. "Amber?"

CHAPTER 7

AMBER

J whirl at the sound of my name, pulling in a startled breath when I see Sean standing in the moonlight.

I blurt the first words that spring to mind for anyone caught doing something they shouldn't be. "I can explain."

He stares at me a moment, then shakes his head in disbelief. He ambles toward me, slow and deliberate, like he's moving though quicksand in a gorilla suit. His expression is somewhere between bemusement and disbelief, and he's mumbling something that sounds like, *"...get my eyes checked."*

"What?"

He lifts a hand, and for a second I think he's reaching for me. But no, he's only grazing the sleeve of my pale pink fleece. "This," he says, rubbing the form-fitting fabric between his fingertips. "Flesh-colored. I thought you were—uh—" He clears this throat. "Never mind."

I look down at my jacket, not sure why we're discussing my fashion choices when I've been caught red-handed trespassing on his property. "It's from Patagonia's new spring line," I supply. "The color's called 'Au Naturel.'"

"You don't say."

I lick my lips, hyper-aware that the last time I saw him, I was pressed braless against his chest with his mouth on mine. "Um, look—I know I'm not supposed to be here, and I should have asked, but I didn't want to bother anyone and—what are you doing?"

"Sitting down." He peels off his jacket and spreads it on the grass like a blanket, then eases himself to the ground. With his back to a willow, he stretches his long legs out in front of him and tilts his face to the sky. "Join me?"

I hesitate, not sure what's happening here. Am I supposed to stay or go?

"Stay," he says without looking at me, making me wonder if I asked my question aloud. I didn't, but I sit down anyway and stretch my legs out next to his. Mine are much shorter, but our knees bump together in the middle, and his body heat warms me through my jeans.

"So what brings you out here?" he asks.

I let a breath out slowly, trying to think of how to explain. "It's stupid."

That gets a small smile from him, though he still doesn't look at me. He seems transfixed by the stars. "I haven't met my quota of stupid yet today, so lay it on me."

I tip my head back to survey the sky overhead. A zillion stars are smeared out across the inky surface like speckles of glitter on black felt. I spend a few seconds locating the big dipper before I reply.

"There's a tree on the other side of the pond," I say. "I don't remember which one, but I wanted to see if my initials are still there."

"Initials?"

A tickle of shame bubbles in my chest. "I carved them. That night I was skin—uh, swimming?"

The corners of Sean's mouth tilt up a little more. "Yeah?"

My cheeks are hot, and I'm hopeful he can't see them in the

69

semi-darkness. "Right. My initials and some guy I was dating back then. I'm not even positive I remember his last name. Jensen or Johnson or something."

He lifts one eyebrow, still not looking at me. "But you were serious enough to deface a tree for him?"

"I was eighteen."

He nods like that's an answer, but I know it's not. "What made you come looking for it tonight?"

I shrug and fiddle with a frayed patch on the knee of my jeans. "Being in the chapel the other day—seeing my grandparents' initials—I guess I started wondering about mine."

"I see."

I wonder if he does. There's a sour bubble of shame in my throat, and I swallow hard to force it back. "I told you it was stupid."

"Not stupid," he says slowly, turning to look at me finally. "We all have relationships that don't work out. It's normal to circle back to the wreckage every now and then to figure out what the hell went wrong."

I nod, impressed by both his turn of phrase and the fact that he seems to get it. I bite my lip, hesitating. "You said you were engaged once?"

"Yep."

"But not married?"

"Nope."

From his one-word answers—and the fact that he's gone back to looking at the sky—I'm guessing he doesn't want to talk about it. I let the subject drop, figuring it's just as well, since I'm bristling with a jealousy I have no right to feel. Still, I'm curious. What sort of woman would Sean Bracelyn pledge to marry? I can't picture him with a waifish model, being a chef and all, though I'm sure women like that throw their twiggy bodies at him all the time. Maybe the daughter of some East Coast million-aires from old money? And what happened, anyway? Did she leave him for a tattooed bad boy or was it a mutual falling out or—

"She died." Sean's words shatter my thoughts so hard I feel glass shards in my throat. "Sarah—that was my fiancée—she passed away."

"Oh, God." I bring my hands to my mouth, kicking myself for bringing this up at all. *Idiot.* I hesitate, then slowly lower one hand and rest it on his knee. "Sean, I'm so sorry. I had no idea. You don't have to talk about it if you don't want."

"It's okay." He takes a deep breath, and I catch myself matching it. We sit there like that for a few beats, breathing in and out together while I wait to see if there's more he wants to share. Should I try to change the subject or wait to see if he does?

When Sean speaks again, his voice is softer. "She was killed in a plane crash," he says. "On her way to visit me in Paris where I was teaching a workshop at Le Cordon Bleu."

"How awful." I press my lips together and shake my head, trying to come up with something to say that doesn't sound trite and hollow. "I can't imagine."

"It's been four years, so I guess I've had time to process it. Want to know the worst part?"

I shake my head, not sure I do. How much worse could it be? A dead fiancée whose only reason for being on the crashed plane was a journey to see the love of her life.

Sean's still looking at me, so I force a response from my achy throat. "Only if you want to share."

"She'd just broken up with me," he says slowly. "Called off the engagement and the wedding and everything. Said I was too closed off, and she couldn't be with someone who didn't know how to open up emotionally."

I study the side of his face, noticing the way the moonlight glints off the cinnamon stubble lining his jaw. I'm not sure I'm following the story. "But she was flying to see you?"

He nods. "Because I asked her to," he says. "I begged her to give us another shot. Sent her a first-class plane ticket and everything. I promised her this big, romantic weekend in Paris with dinner at all the best restaurants and shopping along Avenue Montaigne and the flea markets."

Tears prick the back of my eyelids, but I refuse to let them fall. That's the last thing he needs. "I can't even begin to guess what it would feel like to live through that," I say slowly. "But I'm sorry. So, *so* sorry."

He nods and drops a hand to his thigh, and that's when I realize my hand is still on his leg. I start to draw back, feeling foolish, but Sean folds his hand around mine and laces our fingers together.

He turns to face me, and there's an intensity in those green eyes that steals my breath. "It wouldn't have worked out," he says softly. "With Sarah, I mean. I regret that I didn't let go sooner."

His words make me pause. He regrets not ending things, rather than not opening up the way she wanted him to? I know he said tough conversations aren't his thing, but that seems major.

"Anyway, it's done," he says softly.

So is this conversation, his words seem to signal. But he doesn't look away.

And something in me isn't quite ready to drop it, either.

"You can't blame yourself," I say. "It's easy to have twenty-twenty hindsight after you know how it all shakes out."

"True enough." Sean nods but doesn't take his eyes from mine. Not yet anyway. He's still holding my hand, and he gives it a soft squeeze before turning to look at the sky again. "We had matching tattoos."

"You and Sarah?" There's that spear of jealousy again. I swallow it back and turn my gaze back to the stars.

"Yeah. Not matching, I guess. Complementary. Peanut butter toast for me, jelly for her."

"Seriously?" I catch myself starting to smile, and Sean glances at me with a wry look of his own.

"Yep. It was supposed to be this symbolic tribute to our opposite natures and foodie culture and—hell, I don't know what we were thinking, actually." He shrugs. "Anyway, far be it from me to judge you for carving up a tree."

"There's some perspective." I lift my free hand from the ground beside me and trace a fingertip over the back of Sean's knuckles. He's still holding my other hand, and his fingers tighten around mine. "Where's your tattoo?" I ask.

"Left shoulder. It's small. I'll show it to you sometime if you want."

"I'd like that." I'd love it, actually. The thought of Sean without a shirt sends sizzling little zaps of pleasure from my belly to my fingertips, and I wonder if he feels it in my hands.

We fall silent, both of us tuned to the far-off yip of coyotes and the unseasonably warm breeze caressing our skin.

"This is nice," he says. "I can't believe how warm it is for this time of year."

"It's like this a lot in the high desert. We can have two feet of snow one week and crocuses coming up the next."

He turns to look at me again, and I wonder if I could ever get tired of losing myself in those deep green eyes. "Did you find the tree?"

I'd almost forgotten why I came here tonight. "The one I carved my initials in?" I shake my head. "Nope."

"And the guy?"

"Not really interested in finding him. I haven't seen him for years."

I hesitate, not sure how much more to tell him. But he did just open up with his story, so I find myself spilling my own. "I guess all this wedding planning has me thinking about relationships. About my parents and grandparents and why some people live happily ever after and others just fizzle out. Like, what makes the difference?"

He looks at me oddly for a second. "Work."

There's such certainty in his voice that it takes me by surprise. "Not fate or true love or serendipity or whatever?"

He shakes his head, looking down at our intertwined fingers on his lap. He lifts his free hand and skims a fingertip over my knuckles. It's the gentlest touch, but something about it sends pulses of fire up my arm.

"I don't think so," he says slowly. "The only difference between couples who make it and the ones who don't is a decision to dig in your heels and fight for it."

"Huh." It's an interesting theory. Is that how it was for my grandparents? Or my parents, for that matter.

"But what the hell do I know?" He laughs, but it's a stiff sort of laughter that doesn't reach his eyes. "I'm the unmarried offspring of a guy who should have bought a discount punch-card for divorces. I've never even kept a plant alive, let alone a marriage." He gives me a sweetly self-conscious smile. "I have been thinking about a cat, though."

"A cat?" I blink at him. "Really?"

"Why is that hard to believe?"

"No, it's not that. It's just that we're neutering a whole a bunch of feral cats tomorrow."

Sean frowns. "Please tell me this isn't part of the Testicle Festival."

I laugh, conscious of how often our conversations seem to turn to testicles. Is that my doing?

"It's a clinic we do twice a year at the ranch," I explain. "Jade spays and neuters barn cats and strays and stuff."

"What, with farm tools or something?"

That makes me snort. "Jade's a licensed vet. She mostly just treats our animals, but she does these clinics a few times a year to help keep stray cat colonies down."

"Are any of them up for adoption?"

There's something adorably childlike in his expression, and I focus on that so I'm not overwhelmed by the parts of him that are most definitely not childlike. Broad shoulders, scruffy jawline, a big hand still wrapped around mine.

"Yeah," I tell him. "I mean, some of the feral ones are pretty wild, but we also get a lot of house-cats that someone turned loose in the country."

Sean's brow furrows. "Who'd do something like that?"

"Assholes," I mutter. "Or people who fool themselves into thinking their fluffy little pet who's been totally dependent on them for food and shelter can magically fend for himself in the wilderness."

"God, I hate that." Sean shakes his head. "Do you need volunteers or anything? For the clinic?"

"We can always use an extra set of hands." I do my best not to stare at Sean's hands. "And that will give you first dibs on adoptable cats."

"Deal." Sean grins. "What time should I be there?"

"The clinic opens at eight, but we start getting cats as early as six."

"Six," he repeats, and I'm reminded that Sean's still pretty new to ranch life. That he didn't grow up milking cows at the butt-crack of dawn. I'm not sure he realizes he's volunteering for a day of scrot-snipping just for a free cat, but I decide not to point that out.

"You don't have to come that early," I assure him. "You can do a half-day or just—"

"No, I'll be there," he says. "I can bring breakfast for the volunteers."

"That would be amazing." I smile up at him, wondering if he knows how much I want him to kiss me again.

Either he knows or he's a damn good guesser, because he lowers his mouth to mine and skims a light kiss over my lips. It's soft like the last one, but different somehow. There's an unde-fined tenderness that wasn't there before. I lean back against the tree, the bark rough against my spine as my fingers take on a life of their own and reach up to graze the scruff on Sean's cheek.

He deepens the kiss, threading his fingers through my hair. Our hands are still twined together, but he lifts his free one to my hip. Everything in my body begs him to move up, to slide just a few inches to skim the edge of my breast.

When he does, I gasp out loud. "God," I groan, urging him on with a tilt of my hips.

He obliges, his large palm curving over my not-so-large breast, creating an enormously-large burst of pleasure in the center of my chest. I press into him, hungry for his touch. He tastes like red wine and truffle salt and desire, and I could seriously devour this man.

"God, Amber," he murmurs, trailing kisses down the line of my throat. "What is it about you?"

It seems like a rhetorical question, but I wonder what the answer is. Does he feel the same connection I do?

His fingers catch the zipper on my fleece jacket, and never in my life have I been so grateful to be wearing a v-neck T-shirt. He tugs down the zipper as his kisses inch lower, his breath warm between my breasts.

He eases me back, and I pull him with me, letting my spine settle against the down-filled warmth of his jacket. His hand inches beneath my T-shirt, and even though I'm expecting it, I still moan when his fingers graze my breast.

"You're missing something here," he murmurs, pressing a kiss between my breasts. "Again."

"Right," I murmur, gasping as his mouth claims more territory to the left. "All my bras are in the wash." Because yes, that bra *did* stink. "I—uh—wasn't expecting to see anyone out here."

"Lucky me."

Lucky *me*, I think as his thumb skims my bare nipple, and I arch up to meet the pleasure.

"You're so soft," he murmurs, lowering his head to draw the

stiff peak into his mouth. I groan and clutch the back of his head, willing him to keep going. His tongue makes a slow circuit around my nipple, driving me mad. Every ion in my body shrieks "we want him!" and I bite my lip to keep from screaming it out loud.

This is crazy. How did I get from "let's keep it professional" to clenching his hair in my fist as his mouth devours my bare breasts under the stars? I don't know, but I do know I don't want him to stop. I breathe in the scent of sage and pond water and something I think might be Sean's aftershave, positive I've never wanted anything this badly in my life.

Sean draws back and plants a soft kiss at the top of my breast. It's softer than the last, and there's something in it that feels like the period at the end of a sentence. When his eyes meet mine, there's something in them I can't read.

"We should stop," he whispers.

"We should?"

He nods, and I wonder what the hell I did to spin the car a hundred-and-eighty degrees. "I don't want to," he says. "But this isn't the place for it."

I swallow hard, wondering if he means geographic location or something else. His cabin can't be more than half a mile from here, so I don't think we're talking logistics.

I feel him pulling away, even though he hasn't moved a muscle. "We're both in a weird place right now," I agree, then want to kick myself for uttering such a stupidly benign phrase. I sound like a contestant on *The Bachelor*. Did I do something to scare him off?

When Sean smiles, there's something a little sad in his expression. "I've wanted this forever," he admits. "So I think we can wait until the right time and place and—"

"Right, yes, for sure." I sit up and tug down the hem of my shirt, not sure how to read him right now. Is this really about time and place, or did he change his mind about me?

His gaze holds mine for a few heartbeats, and I have my answer. *He wants me.* He wants me as much as I want him. Longing, sharp and hot, floods my chest so I can hardly breathe. He closes the space between us and kisses me again. Slowly, softly, with aching sweetness.

Then he draws back and gets to his feet, pulling me with him. His hand is still wrapped around mine, and a quick glance at the front of his jeans confirms he's as turned on as I am.

"Okay, I'm stopping for real." He gives me a sheepish smile. "Before I can't."

"Right." I nod toward the bank of trees where I parked my truck. "I'm just over there, so I'll be going now."

"Let me walk you to it."

I shake my head, knowing exactly how that would go. I'm no stranger to fumbling sex on the bench seat of my work truck with boys I have no business fooling around with.

But Sean's no boy, and I think he might be right about something. This isn't the time or place. My brain is still clouded with lust, but there's one thing I'm sure of—I want things to be different with Sean.

"I'm fine," I tell him. "It's fifty feet, and I have a gun in my pocket."

"Jesus." He shakes his head slowly, looking at me like he's never seen me before. "Why is that sexy?"

I laugh and pull back, needing to put some distance between us before I climb him like a jungle gym. "Because you're a city boy," I tell him. "And anything different is exciting and exotic."

And then the shine wears off. I've seen it before, which is why I take another step back. "Good night, Sean."

"Good night, Amber."

I turn and walk away, everything in my body screaming at me not to.

Everything except my heart, which tells me to get the hell in the truck and drive away.

CHAPTER 8

SEAN

I expect to slip out the next morning without an interrogation from my mother, but no such luck.

"Where on earth are you going at this hour?" She glides from her bedroom into the living area wearing a silk robe that looks like something out of a film from the forties. Her eyes are red-rimmed, and I wonder if she was up late.

"Sorry to wake you," I mumble, not really answering the question as I shove food into the cooler I'm packing to take to the reindeer ranch.

My mother steps closer and grabs one of my foil-wrapped breakfast burritos. Without unwrapping it, she lifts it to her face and inhales. "Mmmm. You're still making my famous chicken sausage with garlic and sage."

I nod and finish packing a big bunch of grapes into a tote. "I've made a few modifications to the recipe. You can have that one if you want it."

She eyes me for a moment, then sets the burrito down. "I thought I'd see if Breann is free today to give me a tour of this place. I'd like to see where my grandparents' house used to be."

Bile rises sour in my throat, but I swallow it back to reply.

"Bree has meetings all day. If you wait for me, I can give you a tour when I get back. We'll have plenty of time."

I have no idea if that's true, but I know I want to minimize the time my mother spends around my siblings. Or anyone, for that matter.

"I've been wanting to reorganize your spice cabinet," she says. "I could do that."

"Perfect." I grit my teeth, not wanting my spices reorganized, but figuring it's a small price to pay to keep my mother busy. "I'll make us a late lunch and can give you a tour afterward."

"That sounds lovely." She smiles, and I realize this is the first time I've seen my mother without makeup since I was a boy. She's pretty, maybe prettier than I remember. Fine lines have set around her eyes, and I wonder if the smoothness of her forehead is the result of good genes or a good surgeon.

I heft the cooler off the counter and wonder what it would feel like to hug her right now. We're so unaccustomed to displays of affection that she'd probably have a stroke. "Enjoy your morning," I tell her. "Help yourself to anything in the kitchen."

I hope I won't regret that one. She smiles and adjusts the sash on her robe. "You have a good day."

My drive to the ranch is a short one, and my head is filled with thoughts of Amber. I know I should be more concerned about my mother, but I can't get Amber out of my head. Part of me regrets stopping the other night. Making love to her under the stars would have been a fantasy come true.

But part of me is glad we just talked. Well, talked and groped, but mostly talked. It's rare for me to open up to anyone like I did with her, and I can't put my finger on why it happened.

I'm still thinking about it as I step out of my truck and follow the red and white signs that say, "snip clinic." They lead to a small, modern-looking outbuilding on the other side of the barn. A sign on the door says, "come in," so I push through it and step into an impressively modern-looking vet clinic. The walls are painted white and lined with stainless steel shelves and banks of wire-doored kennels. There's a strong scent of antiseptic, but it's a clean smell that contrasts pleasantly with juniper and hay.

"Hey." Amber smiles as she looks up from her station at the head of a massive stainless-steel table. It's large enough to hold a reindeer, but right now it's holding something much smaller.

"Cute cat," I manage, trying to ignore the way Amber's tugging its crotch like she's hunting for bugs. What the hell is happening? "Is this where I make an appointment to get snipped?"

Jade glances up from the other side of the table and smirks. "You laugh, but I actually had a classmate try that my second year in vet school."

"On himself or someone else?"

"Himself," Amber says. "I remember that story. He couldn't afford a vasectomy, so he tried a do-it-yourself job."

"Ouch." I'm not sure if I'm more squeamish about the story or the fact that Amber's still pulling out the cat's crotch fur in alarming clumps. "Did it work?"

"Nope." Jade draws a scalpel out of some gadget that says "autoclave" on the side, and I try not to think about what she plans to do with it. "He got through the epidermis and had to drive himself to the ER."

I shake my head, ready to change the subject. "Okay, can one of you please tell me what you're doing to that cat? Because to me it looks like you're just ripping fur off his crotch with your bare hands."

"Pretty much." Amber tosses a ball of fine fluff into a waste-basket behind her. "We're plucking the fur from the incision site."

"Can I buy you some razors next time?" I ask. "Please?"

"They irritate the skin," Jade says. "And you definitely don't want irritation where you're about to stick a scalpel."

"I suppose not," I agree, wondering for the millionth time what else I don't know about life on a ranch.

Finally reaching the end of her task, Amber stands up and leaves her sister to—uh, I don't want to consider what Jade's about to do. I keep my focus on Amber and the delight that's flooding her face. I'd like to pretend it's me, but I'm guessing she's just hungry.

"You really brought breakfast?" she says. "Oh my God, I love you."

I know she's kidding, and it's not the first time a woman I barely know has professed undying affection over my culinary skills. Still, the words leave me flush with happiness. So does the sweater she's wearing. It's red and fitted and even though the neckline isn't low, it offers a stunning view of the curves beneath it. Curves I had my hands on less than twelve hours ago.

I order myself to stop gawking at her and feed her instead. Prying the top off the cooler, I show her the tidy foil-wrapped bundles inside. "I wasn't sure how many people you'd have or how the shifts would work, so I packed a couple dozen breakfast burritos you can microwave one at a time."

"Oh my God, that smells amazing. Are they still warm?"

"They should be. Do you have time to sit?"

"For sure," she says. "Jade could totally do a castration in her sleep."

"Let's hope she doesn't, since my cousin sleeps here a lot."

Amber laughs and turns to scrub her hands at a large stainless-steel sink. Wiping them on a paper towel, she moves toward a tiny card table tucked under a window in the corner. "You doing okay, Jade?" she calls.

"Peachy keen," she calls. "Save one of those for me."

Amber sits down on one side of the table and takes the foil-wrapped burrito I hand her. I glance back at the unconscious tabby Jade is leaning over on the other side of the room. For the first time I notice he's missing his right rear leg. "What's the story with that cat?"

"Stray," Amber says as she peels away the wrapper and dunks

her burrito in the small cup of salsa I've just handed her. "Someone dumped him here a week ago. He's a surprisingly good mouser considering the missing wheel."

"Why would somebody just leave a three-legged cat?" I shake my head, disgusted by my fellow humans. "Or any cat, for that matter."

"It happens a lot." Amber finishes swishing her burrito in the salsa. "People get tired of being responsible for a pet, so they drive them out into the country."

"They think they're 'setting them free,'" Jade calls, not bothering to mask her disgust.

"Mostly they become coyote food," Amber admits. "The lucky ones find their way here."

I steal a glance back at the operating table, then wish I hadn't. If this one's lucky, I don't want to know what unlucky looks like.

"What's going to happen to him?" I ask. "Do you turn him loose again or what?"

Amber shrugs and reaches for the salsa. "We're full up on barn cats right now, so we'll try to find him a home. Why, are you interested?"

"Maybe." I don't know why, but I feel an odd kinship with the three-legged cat. True, we haven't met, but I feel for the guy.

A crippling urge to rescue.

That's what Sarah used to call it, but I don't think that's what's driving me. Besides, there's nothing wrong with wanting to help someone. To take a shitty situation and make it better.

Amber bites into her burrito, then closes her eyes and gives a reverent moan. "Oh my God, this is amazing," she says around a mouthful of food. "What's in this?"

I'm distracted by the blissed-out look on her face and almost forget to answer. "Homemade chicken sausage with sage and garlic, a little kale, sweet potato, organic eggs, smoked gouda, caramelized onions—"

"Good Lord, why have I never made friends with a chef

before this?" She grins at me, and I try not to hang up on the word "friends." Is she in the habit of groping other friends? It's none of my business, but jealousy nips the edges of my heart anyway.

She takes another bite and sighs with pleasure, and I can't help remembering those same sighs last night. What would it have been like if I hadn't hit the brakes? Part of me regrets it, but part of me knows it was the smart move.

"Next time you meet a girl you like, do her a favor." Sarah's long-ago words ring in my head, echoes of what she said to me before she kicked my ass to the curb. *"Let her see the real Sean sometime. Not Prep School Sean. Not Damage Control Sean. The* real *Sean."*

As I watch Amber devour the burrito, I'm positive I'm getting there. Maybe it's her zest for life. Maybe it's her kooky humor or her kindness toward animals or her passion for food. Maybe I'm just really, *really* hot for her.

It's all of those things in Amber that bring out the best version of me.

She must sense me staring at her with a way-too-serious expression because she gestures to the burrito and does a mock swoon. "This is seriously like the best thing I've ever put in my mouth," she says. "Ever."

"Says the girl who used to put marbles in her mouth," Jade calls from the operating table.

"What? I wanted to see what they tasted like." Amber grins and takes another bite of burrito.

"Please tell me you were three and not twenty-three."

Amber laughs and dumps more salsa on her burrito, then moans as she takes another bite. "So good."

"You're making me uncomfortable with all that groaning over there," Jade calls.

"Says the girl whose bedroom is down the hall from mine." Amber gives me a pointed look. "Brandon stays over a lot."

I glance over at Jade to see her blushing bright pink over her surgical mask. I can't tell if she's smiling, but I'm guessing she might be.

"You guys have the best relationship."

"Family's weird," she agrees cheerfully. "Gotta love 'em, though."

I consider telling her about my mother. About the drama with her showing up at the ranch and the awkwardness with my siblings. I wonder if there are any hot-button issues with her parents, and I open my mouth to start the conversation.

But I close it again quickly.

No. Not now. Mid-castration is hardly the time for a deep-digging conversation about family. In the back of my head, my dead ex-fiancée tells me I'm doing it again, but I push her voice aside and push a pile of napkins toward Amber.

"Stumpy the cat should be awake in a few hours if you want to meet him," Amber says. "By then we'll have a whole bunch of other cats here for you to check out."

"Thanks." I fish into the cooler for another burrito, not interested in the other cats. I know Stumpy's going home with me, though he might do it with another name.

Jade finishes the snip job and joins us on the other side of the room. I set her up with a burrito and her own cup of salsa while she washes up at the big sink before dragging another chair over to the table.

I hand her the foil wrapped package, and she wastes no time peeling it open. "You guys are killing me with these," she says before taking a bite. "Holy crap, you're right. He's amazing."

"See?" Amber grins at me, a smile that shoots straight to my groin. I could never get tired of feeding this woman. I make a mental note to do it as often as possible.

"I aim to please." I shove a pile of napkins at Jade as Amber polishes off her burrito and glances at her watch.

"We've got ten minutes until everyone else shows up, so eat fast," Amber says.

Jade chews more quickly and nods at her sister. "Did you figure out what you're doing tomorrow?"

Amber makes a face. "Not yet. I'm still considering my options."

"What's tomorrow?" I ask.

Amber dabs her mouth with a napkin. "A wedding I'm supposed to go to. I was planning to go with this guy friend of mine, but he just bailed."

"Friend." Jade snorts and dunks her burrito in the salsa. "Connor would polish your shoes with his tongue if you asked."

"Not true," Amber says, looking embarrassed. "And since he has the flu, I don't want his tongue anywhere near me."

There's a flicker of jealousy at the center of my chest, and I do my best to ignore it. "So are you just going to go stag, or what?"

Amber shrugs and takes another sip of coffee. "I'd rather not go at all, honestly."

"You have to," Jade says. "You promised Beth."

"Right, my spy mission." Amber rolls her eyes and wipes her hand on a napkin. "Beth used to date the groom."

"She's over him, obviously." Jade takes another bite of burrito.

"Sure," I agree. "I send spies to the weddings of all my ex-girl-friends."

"She wants to know about his wedding," Amber says. "So she doesn't accidentally make hers too similar."

"Or so she can make hers better," Jade scoffs. "I'm glad I'm in charge of reindeer and not all the wedding stuff. Some of these brides are nuts."

Amber just shrugs and balls up her foil. "It's human nature to be curious about exes. Can't blame a girl for wondering."

"No, but I can blame her for being a stalker," Jade says. "She doesn't expect you to bring back video or anything like that, does she?"

Amber shakes her head. "Just a detailed report."

I ball up my own burrito foil and add it to Amber's. "Want me to go with you?"

Both sisters look at me. "To the wedding?" Jade asks.

I nod. "Sure, if you want a date."

"I want," Amber says with surprising enthusiasm. "Seriously?"

I shrug, trying not to look too eager. "It's a good chance to scope out what local caterers are doing for weddings."

"I thought you weren't interested in doing weddings," Amber says.

She's got me there. "Okay, it's a good chance to see you in a short dress," I admit. "Maybe something blue. Or no, yellow."

Across the table, Jade smirks. "With cleavage," she adds helpfully.

Amber rolls her eyes. "Would you two like to just take over my closet and dress me?"

Jade shoots me a look that says she knows exactly what I'm thinking. That *undressing* Amber is more what's on my mind. She's got me there, but I do my best to keep my eyes off the front of Amber's red sweater. To convince big sister Jade I'm not one of those guys who's only after one thing.

In any case, one thing's for sure: I've never been more eager to attend a damn wedding.

* * *

MY MOTHER WALKS in and sniffs when she sees me crouching in front of the fireplace the next morning, stroking a hand down my new cat's back. I've set up a small recovery ward for him, though he already shredded the fancy cat bed I bought while he was still groggy from anesthesia.

For now, he seems happy lying in a box marked "frozen halibut cheeks."

Okay, "happy" is a relative term.

"Is it growling or purring?" my mother asks.

"Growling," I admit. "But I'll win him over eventually."

She eyes the scratches on my arms and sniffs again. "You always were determined. I'll give you that much."

I can't tell from her tone if it's a compliment or a complaint, so I respond with a grunt. "He'll come around."

"I suppose I'm not surprised you picked a cat with a missing leg," she says. "You always were a softie."

Now I'm really not sure about the whole compliment/complaint thing, so I just keep petting my cat. "He needed help, and I needed a cat. It's a symbiotic thing."

My mother mumbles something that sounds like "co-dependent," but I might be hearing things. "Does he have a name?" she asks.

"Gordon," I reply. "Gordon Ramsay."

That earns me a laugh. "He's got the attitude."

Gordon opens one eye and peers at my mother. He gives another growl and closes it again

"It probably has fleas," my mother says.

"No fleas in the high desert," I point out. "It's too cold at night."

I learned that from Amber, along with a dozen other bits of animal-related trivia I picked up yesterday at the ranch. If the occasion arises for me to regale prep school classmates with knowledge of reindeer mating habits, I'll be ready.

"Shouldn't you be getting ready for the wedding?"

I straighten up and smooth my hands down the lapels of my suit jacket. I'm ninety percent sure I'm overdressed for a small-town Oregon wedding, but the look on my mother's face suggests I'm not quite up to her standards.

She glides forward to reach for my tie. "It's crooked," she says. "And much too loose."

"Ow!" I slip a finger under the fabric as she yanks it tight.

She pats my hand away. "You never could do a proper

Windsor knot. I don't know what they were teaching you at that prep school."

"Math, science, and literature?"

"They were supposed to be teaching you *manners*," she says. "I did my best, you know."

Her gaze lifts to mine and holds for a few beats. For just a moment, I think she might say something sentimental.

"I spoke with my lawyer this morning."

And that's as sentimental as she gets.

"Oh?" I try for nonchalant, but the truth is that I'm nervous about the stack of paperwork that showed up via Fed Ex yesterday.

"Just trying to get things straightened out with the title," she says. "Making sure you kids have proper claim to the land and all that."

"So you're looking out for us," I say slowly.

She meets my eye and gives a curt nod. "Exactly. Just trying to do what's right."

I clear my throat and wonder if that's mouthwash I smell on her breath. It reminds me of the peppermint schnapps I bought for a chocolate torte last Christmas, and I try to recall where I shoved the bottle.

My mother steps back and surveys her handiwork with a critical eye. The Windsor knot or her son, I'm not sure which. "You'd better get going so you're not late."

I nod and take my own step back, putting a familiar distance between us. "You'll keep an eye on Gordon?"

She looks down at the floor as though I've just entrusted her with folding a pile of laundry. Then she sighs.

"To the best of my abilities, of course."

"Of course."

I give my tie a tug, then turn and walk out of the room, ignoring the growing sense of dread in the pit of my gut.

CHAPTER 9

AMBER

*H*oly Mother of Cheesecake, Sean Bracelyn looks good in a suit. I somehow refrained from drooling on his lapels for the drive to the wedding venue, but just barely.

"How about I pull up in front of the church so you can hop out?" he suggests.

"Embarrassed to be seen with me?" I tease.

Sean snorts and lifts his sunglasses to look me in the eye. "I've already called all the paparazzi I know to make sure I'm photographed with you as much as possible. I want documentation of that time I went out with the hottest girl in the universe."

I laugh and toss my hair over one shoulder. "Do you actually know any paparazzi?"

"No," he admits. "But I might have to find some. Seriously, you look smokin'."

I should probably demur, crossing my legs and murmuring, "this old thing?" like some Hollywood actress. But the truth is that I do look good. I don't get a lot of chances to dress up on the farm, so I used Greg's wedding as an excuse to buy an Adrianna Papell rose lace sheath dress at Nordstrom Rack the last time I was in Portland. The cap sleeves and v-neck show off my shoulders, and the Badgley Mischka peep-toe heels I got for a song make my legs look killer.

But they're not the most comfortable footwear on earth, which is why I appreciate Sean's offer to drop me off in front of the church. "Thank you," I say as he pulls the car up to the curb. "I'll get us a good seat."

He grins and flips up the visor. "I'll come find you."

I step out of the car and make my way up the steps to the church, surveying the crowd for someone I know. I spot a couple women from Jade's graduating class and try to recall if they're among the assholes who bullied her mercilessly in high school. I was five years behind her and didn't find out about the bullying until recently, so I've been making up for lost time by despising my sister's tormentors extra hard.

"Amber! Over here."

I turn to see a group of more familiar faces near the front of the church. There's a cluster of my high school soccer teammates standing to the left of the door, and I make my way over to them.

"Angie," I say, doling out the requisite hugs. "And Kinsey, oh my God, when are you due?"

"Three more weeks." My old friend beams and strokes her massive belly. "I feel like I'm incubating a walrus."

"I have such baby fever every time I see you," Blanka Pavlo gushes in her faint Ukrainian accent. She came to Oregon our junior year as an exchange student and ended up moving back after college. "I can't wait 'til it's my turn."

"Might want to find a husband first," Angie says, giving her a teasing wink. "Or a boyfriend."

"Totally overrated." Lily Archer grins and stretches across Kinsey's belly to give me a tight hug. "Flings are better anyway. Speaking of which, who was that crazyhawt guy who dropped you off?"

"Please say he's single," Angie pleads, glancing the direction Sean's car disappeared. "Or that he has five or six brothers who are single?"

"Uh, actually—" I give them a knowing smirk, enjoying the way their jaws fall open. "There are at least three or four brothers that I've heard of. I don't know their marital status, but judging by the DNA pool, I'm guessing they're not bad to look at. You know Brandon, right?"

Blanka nods. "Your sister's husband?"

"Technically they're not married yet, but yes. His cousins are the ones who own Ponderosa Luxury Ranch Resort."

Kinsey fans herself with a wedding program. "It's not open yet, is it?"

"Almost," I tell her. "Sean is a chef. He's the one in charge of all the restaurant stuff for the resort. There's also a sister in charge of marketing and—"

"Forget the sister." Lily gives me a wicked smile. "Tell us about the brothers."

"And Sean," Angie adds. "Or is he yours?"

This is the precise moment Sean comes jogging up the steps, earning a startled titter from the ladies. The smile he gives me suggests he's just heard every word Angie said, and that he's waiting for the answer.

"Uh, he's my date for this," I stammer. "Sean, this is Angie, Kinsey, Blanka, and Lily. We played soccer together in high school."

"Ladies." Sean gives a friendly nod and rests a hand on the small of my back. It's a chaste enough touch, but it sends goose bumps rippling up my arms. I take a few breaths and try to regain my composure.

Lily gives me a knowing look and turns toward the door. "Come on. Let's get a good seat up front."

I follow my friends down the aisle with Sean at my side like the world's most delicious piece of arm candy. Is it wrong that I love seeing envy on the faces of several former classmates as we make our way to an empty row near the middle of the church?

As we settle into the pews, I survey the rest of the scene. It's less crowded than I expected, considering Greg was one of the more popular kids in my graduating class, though I haven't seen him for at least a year. He went to college back east and settled out there after graduation. The bride is from Tennessee, so I'm not sure why they're having the wedding here.

I remind myself to stop speculating and to focus on observing the wedding details for Beth. Ivory pillar candles flicker inside white painted lanterns at the end of each row, casting a romantic glow on the simple spray of baby's breath tied with tulle bows at the end of each pew. Their colors are cream and cinnamon. Very tasteful and elegant.

I know Beth is hoping I'll come back with something catty to say, but I've got nothing so far.

"Nice place," Sean murmurs. "What's the history?"

"It was built in 1912 as one of the city's first Presbyterian churches," I tell him. "It's changed hands a bunch of times since then, and now it's more of an event center than a church"

"That stone work is incredible."

"It came from an old rock quarry beside the Deschutes River," I tell him. "That's why it's called the Old Stone Church."

"It's amazing." He smiles and leans closer. "So are you. Did I mention I'm nuts about that dress?"

Heat pulses through me, but I fight back a self-satisfied smile. "Once or twice."

His knuckles graze mine in the space between us, and I hold my breath hoping he'll take my hand. "I should probably apologize for presuming you'd need a date to the wedding," he says. "You would have been just fine going stag or with your girlfriends, huh?"

"I would have," I admit, catching a whisper of "so hot" from my friends seated on the other side of me. "But I'm glad you offered."

"So am I," he says.

A change in the music signals the start of the ceremony, so we stop talking and turn our attention to the aisle. The groom strides through the door, dashing in his charcoal tux. He's followed by a pack of groomsmen that includes two of his brothers and a couple guys I don't recognize. Each is paired with a bridesmaid bedecked in floor-length taffeta in sparkling cinnamon. I don't know any of them, but the flower girl I recognize as a niece of the groom. She's chubby-cheeked and adorable, hurling fistfuls of rose petals like a soldier chucking grenades.

Da-da-da-da-da!

The first notes of the wedding march propel us to our feet, and we turn to face the bride standing in the doorway. She grips a bouquet of peach-colored roses in one hand and her father's arm in the other.

I'd never tell Beth, but the bride is a knockout. One of those flawless complexions that looks like she's been airbrushed, and her dark hair cascades down her back in an artful array of ringlets. A photographer clicks off a few shots before ducking into the pew behind us. The bride sails past, her expression serene and lovely.

But it's the groom who gets the biggest smile of all from her. He's absolutely beaming as she covers the distance between them, her bouquet trembling in her hands. As she steps up beside Greg, his eyes glitter with emotion. He mouths the words "You are perfect," and my chest gets tight.

It's a beautiful moment, but I can't help feeling the weight on her shoulders. Thinking about what it's like to have someone look at you as though you hung the moon, and he expects you to keep holding it there until your arms fall off.

"Dearly beloved—"

The minister kicks things off in the usual fashion, with a spiel about good times and bad, about friendship and laughter and joy and sorrow. I'm only half-listening, since I'm hyper-conscious of Sean beside me. He's wearing some sort of woodsy cologne that makes me want to devour him like a cupcake, and his thigh is solid and warm pressed against mine.

"Greg and Alien," the minister drones. "What you're doing here today is—"

Wait, what?

Sean leans close and gives me a puzzled look. "*Alien?* Isn't her name Aline?" he whispers.

I glance down at the program in my lap, scrolling through the rows of flowery script. I slide a thumb down the page until I locate the name *Aline Nicole Andrews* next to the title *Bride*.

"I think so?" I whisper. "This font is a little weird."

"I suppose odds are slim someone named their kid *Alien*."

I bite my lip and try not to giggle. "Let's hope."

Sean squeezes my hand, and I wonder if he's fighting as hard as I am not to bust up laughing.

At the front of the church, the minister drones on. He's at least four hundred years old, and has the glassy-eyed look of a guy who may have knocked back a couple shots of whiskey before the service. From the look of the best man, they may have attended the same happy hour. I hope neither of them passes out before this service ends.

"At this time," the minister says, "Greg and Alien wish to symbolically mark their union with the lighting of the unity candle."

The bride and groom step forward to focus on their fiery task, and if they're fazed by the minister's faux pas, they don't show it. They grip their candles with single-minded determination, moving toward the large pillar that serves as the unity candle.

It's possible they're missing the minister's name flub over the shrill wail of the vocalist posing beside the organ. She's belting out her solo like this is an American Idol audition, and it takes me a second to figure out the song.

"'You Must Love Me,'" I whisper. "Isn't this a Madonna song?"

Sean listens a moment, then nods. "It's from that movie 'Evita.' Isn't it from a scene about her dying?"

"Huh." Okay, so I'm definitely getting fodder to report back to Beth. I almost feel bad about that.

"*You must love me,*" the vocalist sings, then shifts to sotto voice and leans down to the organist. "*Keep going,*" she chirps in a nervous, sing-song voice, "*something's wrong.*"

Sean looks at me. I frown at the singer, pretty sure that's not the line.

I glance from the confused-looking organist to where the bride and groom are struggling with the unity candle. The groom shoves his hand inside the glass holder, and I hold my breath hoping he doesn't get stuck.

"...can't get the wick..." the groom mutters.

A groomsman steps forward and pulls out a pocketknife. I lean close to Sean and stifle a laugh. "You know it's a farm-kid wedding when someone busts out a Leatherman."

He squeezes my hand as the groom finishes digging out the wick, then sets the candle back on the stand.

Please light, I channel silently to the candle. *And please don't catch her veil on fire.*

A small cheer goes up in the audience as the candle finally blazes to life. I look down and realize I've been squeezing Sean's fingers like a goat milking machine. I loosen my grip and breathe a sigh of relief as the bride and groom turn away from the candles and move back to the front of the church.

"I like that," Sean whispers. "That they left their candles burning instead of snuffing them out."

I'm surprised he'd notice such a small detail. "Me, too," I whisper back. "I wonder if it's symbolic or they forgot."

"Let's say symbolic," he says. "It's a cool idea."

It *is* a cool idea, and I feel a pinch of jealousy remembering he was engaged before. How far did he and Sarah get with the planning? Did they talk about things like snuffing their candles versus leaving them lit as a symbol of individuality?

Another ripple of jealousy moves through my chest, which is annoying. Who the hell do I think I am?

"The exchanging of rings is a symbolic ritual that dates back to—"

Sean squeezes my hand. "Uh-oh," he whispers.

"What?"

He nods toward the front of the church. "Is it just me, or does the groom look panicked?"

I glance at Greg, and sure enough, he's white as a ghost. But it's not the look of a man with cold feet. He's clutching the bride's hands in a way that suggests something else is going on.

I wince. "Ten bucks says he forgot the ring."

"Ooof." Sean shakes his head in sympathy as Aline's expression shifts. I'm pretty sure she just figured out what's going on, and she's not thrilled. She mouths something to him, but I can't make out the words. Greg mouths something back and shakes his head.

There's a soft click as someone switches on a microphone, probably anticipating the vows. That's how the whole church is treated to the bride's loud pronouncement:

"I am *not* just going to fake it."

I bring a hand to my mouth, determined not to laugh. I fail when Lily leans over and whispers in my ear. "I am *so* including that line in my vows someday."

I lose it then, which is fine since the rest of the congregation is now chuckling. The helpless groom looks to his best man, then digs in his pocket and hands over his car keys.

Sean turns to watch the best man sprint down the aisle. "I'm impressed by how much stuff these guys have in their pockets."

"Oh, I guarantee at least a few people in this room are packing firearms."

"There's a comforting thought."

The best man hustles out the door, while the bride whispers something to the vocalist. The organ starts up again, and the singer launches into an upbeat rendition of Meghan Trainor's "Dear Future Husband." It's an interesting choice, and I feel a little fluttery when they get to the part about him loving her even when she's acting crazy. Lord knows whoever I marry someday will have his work cut out for him.

My girlfriends are chattering quietly beside us. At one point, Lily catches my eye and points to Sean.

"Hot," she mouths, giving me a thumbs up.

I turn to see Sean smiling down at me. "I love that everyone's being cool about this," he says. "Even the bride and groom are pretty chill."

I swing my gaze back to the front of the church, cheered to see he's right. Greg and Aline are holding hands and sharing the sort of private laughter you only see from couples who really, really dig each other. I've watched my parents do it, and I always hope someday I'll have that for myself.

I don't realize I'm squeezing Sean's hand again until he leans close and brushes the hair from my ear. "That's what I meant," he whispers.

I turn to face him, stomach flipping over at the sight of those green eyes. "What?"

"When I said the secret is work," he whispers. "Getting mad right now would be the easiest thing in the world for them. Blaming someone else? Simple. Doing the opposite is what's hard. It takes work to decide you're going to love someone even when things aren't as perfect as they were in your head."

I swallow hard, not sure when my throat swelled up tight. My eyelids prickle, and I don't know if I'm more moved by this ceremony or by the words Sean's just spoken.

Or maybe it's Sean himself. How long can I keep pretending I'm not falling for him? That this is just a casual flirtation?

I grip his hand, wondering if he feels the same.

The best man comes racing up the aisle with a ring box clutched in his fist. Everyone applauds as he hands it to groom, and the ceremony continues.

I'm sure there are vows in there somewhere, and maybe even another *Alien* reference from the minister, but I hear none of it. All I hear are Sean's words echoing in my mind.

It takes work to decide you're going to love someone even when things aren't as perfect as they were in your head.

I swallow back the lump in my throat, wondering when I got so emotional. I'm not a crier, not by any stretch of the imagination. I glance at Sean, and he gives me a smile that makes my whole chest feel like a puddle of melted candle wax.

"I now pronounce you man and wife," the minister announces. "Ladies and gentlemen, may I present to you Mr. Gregory David Lucas and Mrs. Aline Nicole Andrews-Lucas."

"Ooof," Sean whispers as we get to our feet to watch the newlyweds sail down the aisle.

"What?" I ask. "He said it right that time."

"Yeah, but she hyphenated."

"So?" I'm bristled to argue about a woman's right to keep her name when Sean taps the program in front of me. "I'm guessing they didn't think through her initials."

"Wha—oh. Oh, dear."

Aline Nicole Andrews-Lucas.

ANAL?

I stifle a groan and wave to the newlyweds as they float down the aisle. "Maybe she'll ditch the middle name," I suggest.

The mother of the bride steps up to the pulpit and grabs the microphone. "Ladies and gentlemen, Greg and *Aline—*" heavy emphasis there "—would like to invite you all to proceed to the Father Luke Hall just across the street. The newlyweds will join us just as soon as they've taken their first photographs as husband and wife."

One by one, we file down the aisle and out the doors. I keep hold of Sean's hand, telling myself it's only because I know where we're going and not because I want the excuse to touch him.

"Well that was something else," Angie says as she falls into step beside us.

Kelsey laughs and rubs a hand over her mound of incubating baby. "That's nothing. Remember at my wedding when the best man passed out and knocked that big candelabra into the flowers?"

Blanka groans and shakes her head. "I never got the fire extinguisher goo out of my favorite shoes."

Lily grins and looks at Sean. "You're a real trooper. Amber says you have brothers."

I roll my eyes at my friend's lack of subtlety, but Sean just smiles. "Yep. Gobs of them."

Lily licks her lips, and I wonder if I should warn the Bracelyn brothers that my friend is a verified man-eater.

"Here we are," I announce, pushing through the doorway and into the cozy reception hall bedecked in cream and cinnamon. I survey the tables, each one artfully adorned with tasteful vases of lilies and sand-filled dishes of tealight candles. It's a beautiful setup, and I'm jotting mental notes for Beth when something explodes.

Glass shards ricochet off the walls, and someone gives an ear-shattering shriek. I'm turning away just as something slams into the center of my chest.

I look down and suck in a breath.

Blood. Blood everywhere, though the pain is only a dull ache.

There's another explosion and Lily screams, too. There's blood on her, blood on the tablecloths, blood on the carpet—

"Get down!" Sean doesn't wait for me to obey. He drags me to the floor, throwing himself on top of me so he's shielding my body with his.

There's another explosion and I close my eyes, waiting for the gunfire to stop.

CHAPTER 10

SEAN

*I*t's not gunfire.

That's what I keep telling myself over and over as I wait for the explosions to stop.

I'll admit that's what I thought for the first few seconds, especially after Amber's comment about wedding guests packing heat.

But here's where it comes in handy that I've worked my fair share of weddings gone awry.

"Marinara," I murmur, and Amber opens her eyes.

"What?"

I should probably get off her, since the explosions have stopped. She feels warm and lush beneath me, and I figure I need to stay here a few seconds longer. For safety and all.

I pick up a meatball that's landed next to her head. "Just a guess, but I think a couple chafing dishes exploded. I've seen it before."

Amber stares at the meatball like I'm holding up a human eyeball, then blinks at me. "You've seen this happen?"

"Not this, exactly. It was pulled pork instead of meatballs. Are you okay?"

She nods, looking uncertain. "I think so. Are you?"

"Yeah." Better than okay with Amber's body pressed against mine like this.

She looks down like she's wanting to check herself for damage, but that's tough to do with me lying on top of her.

I roll to the side, then hop to my feet and pull her with me. Her arms are smeared with marinara, and she has gobs of it in her hair. But aside from that, she looks unscathed. She also looks so beautiful my chest aches, and I can't resist the urge to fish half a meatball out of her cleavage.

"Thank you," she breathes.

"You're welcome."

I move toward the table where the food has been set up. Sure enough, there's a charred mess that must have been a pair of old school, retro chafing dishes. "The candles must have overheated. Probably used some that were too big." I turn and survey the room. "Is anyone hurt?"

I get a few dazed head shakes and some serious looks of confusion. My heart is thudding in my ears, and I need to be sure everyone's okay. Since Amber was at the front of the crowd, she bore the brunt of the explosion. I shift my gaze back to her and feel my heart twist in my chest. "You sure you're okay?"

She nods, looking dazed but unhurt. God, if anything happened to her—

"What was that?" someone asks again.

"Chafing dish explosion," I say again, pretty sure I'll be repeating that at least a few more times.

I survey the room and all its pretty décor. There are meatballs smashed against the wall. Meatballs on the ceiling. Meatballs tangled in the curtains. There's even a meatball wedged in the corner of a framed photo of the bride and groom. I pick it off and turn to see a wide-eyed teen in a white apron holding a giant bowl of spinach salad.

"Are you with the catering team?" I ask.

She nods and gapes at the carnage around us. "I swear everything was fine a minute ago. What h—"

"Where's your manager?"

"I—uh—" The kid swallows. "She's not here. She had another wedding to do. We're just supposed to serve the food."

Amber steps up beside me and looks around. "I can't believe no one's hurt. That could have been so much worse."

I survey the rest of the buffet line, surprised to see the carnage isn't as bad as I thought. "The rest of the food looks fine. Good thing everything's covered."

The mother of the bride walks in at that moment, then gasps like she's been punched in the face. "Oh my God! What happened?"

"Chafing dish accident," I tell her when the catering kid says nothing. "The meatballs are a total loss, but everything else should be good. If we can just get some new tablecloths and clean up the glass and—"

"But the meatballs were the main dish." The mother of the bride is close to tears. "We're on a tight budget, so we didn't do the prime rib or the chicken cordon bleu or even the kebabs."

"Right." I survey the room again, wondering how quickly we could get this cleaned up. I turn back to the mother of the bride, who doesn't look too steady on her feet. "What kind of meatballs?"

She blinks. "I—uh—sorry?"

"Beef, pork, chicken?"

Spotting one that's landed neatly in a teacup beside me, I pick it up and study it. "Chicken," I say. "Fresh sage, rosemary, maybe a little bit of thyme."

"Sean is a chef," Amber announces when the mother of the bride stares like I've just announced I eat human ears as snacks.

"That's right," the mother of the bride says slowly. "We got chicken because the groom's mom is a pesco pollo vegetarian."

She twists her hands together in front of her and looks helplessly at the mess. "I don't know what we're going to do now."

I clear my throat, conscious of Amber's hand on my arm, and the fact that the guy in a white chef's hat rarely gets to play the hero.

"You don't always have to save the day," Sarah chides in the back of my head.

But goddamn it, sometimes I do.

I rest my hand on Amber's back and nod to the mother of the bride. "I've got it covered," I say. "Here's the plan."

* * *

THE FACILITY TURNS out to have a surprisingly nice kitchen, and one of the catering kids is dispatched to the gourmet grocery store down the street with a list of ingredients.

I ditch my tie and jacket and don a full-length chef's apron pillaged from a hook behind the door. Then I get to work assembling the tools I'll need. The pantry holds a huge stockpile of D.O.P. Certified San Marzano's tomatoes, which seems like a sign from heaven. There's also a net bag of fresh garlic, so I drag a big chef's knife from the block on the stainless steel counter and start chopping.

Amber pushes through the door as I'm peeling and dicing like a madman, and she stands watching for a moment. "Wow. You're good at that."

"I've had some practice."

Her eyes stay fixed on my hands for a moment before she shakes her head and clears her throat. "The mother of the bride is stalling the newlyweds at their photo shoot," she reports. "The groom's mom rounded up a cleaning crew and is cracking the whip as we speak."

"Perfect." I shove a pile of freshly-chopped garlic to the side and reach for more.

Amber takes a few steps closer and gives one of my apron strings a soft tug. "So this is what a Superman cape looks like in real life."

I smile and use the flat edge of my knife to crush the garlic. "I haven't saved the day yet."

"No, but you will." She smiles and lets go of my apron, boob-grazing my arm in a way I'm pretty sure was deliberate. "Have I mentioned I'm damn glad I brought you as my date?"

"Have I mentioned you look fucking amazing in that dress?" I grin. "Even covered with meatball."

A subtle flush spreads from her chest to her neck, and I have the sudden urge to lick marinara off her cleavage. But there's work to do.

"Any chance I could give you a task?"

"Absolutely," she says. "That's what I came in here for."

"How comfortable would you be grabbing that immersion blender and crushing up the tomatoes?"

"Very comfortable." She picks it up off the counter and turns it around in her hands. "We use one sometimes to make rolled corn cakes as treats for the reindeer. Have you spotted a can opener anywhere?"

"I'm crossing my fingers there's one in the drawer behind you."

She turns and rummages through it, and I order myself to keep my eyes on my knife instead of the lovely view of her ass. The last thing we need right now is a trip to the ER with my severed finger in a cup of ice.

A door swings open and the catering kid comes in lugging four massive bags of groceries. He's breathless as he plunks them down on the closest counter. "I found everything on your list, even the gluten-free breadcrumbs."

"Awesome." I grab one of the bags from him, trying to remember his name. He mentioned earlier that he's a culinary student, and I'm pretty sure it's Josh. "Normally we'd make our own breadcrumbs, but we're a little short on time."

"No kidding," the kid says as he starts to unpack the food.

Amber's busy plugging in the immersion blender, and I try not to notice how much it looks like a vibrator. I tear my eyes off her and focus on the culinary kid, who's watching me like he's planning to take notes on everything I say. "We'd ordinarily want to skip the immersion blender and hand-crush the tomatoes, but that's another time saver."

Amber looks up. "I don't mind using my hands if that's how you'd like me to do it."

My mind veers into the gutter again, but I yank it back and shake my head. "The blender is fine."

She shrugs and flicks the switch, kicking the buzzing device to life. How have I never noticed the phallic shape of a goddamn hand blender?

I force my attention off Amber and turn back to the catering kid, who's unpacking the last of the groceries. "Thanks for grabbing these. Josh, right?"

"Right. Yes, sir. And you're—you're Sean Bracelyn, right? The Sean Bracelyn who won the James Beard Award for Best Chef in the northeast region. And isn't your mother the—"

"Just Sean is good," I interrupt, not wanting to head down that path. "You found the dried porcini mushrooms."

He nods a little shyly and pushes the bag across the counter. "They had fresh ones, too, but—"

"No, dried is what you want here," I tell him. "You've gotta grind them yourself for optimal flavor."

"Really?" The kid steps closer, intrigued, and I remember what it felt like to be a wide-eyed newbie in culinary school. "Do you use a mortar and pestle or what?"

"Sure, or a spice grinder will do," I tell him. "The main thing is to get them nice and fine so they add an earthy depth."

"Cool." He offers a hopeful smile. "Can I help?"

"How are your herb chopping skills?" I ask.

"Good." He grins. "I just finished an entry-level knife skills class."

"Then you can rinse off that chef's knife and get to work on those. Parsley, sage, basil, thyme, rosemary—cutting board is over there, and we want them nice and fine."

"I'm on it." Josh sets to work, while Amber continues whirring away with the blender in a giant bowl of tomatoes. She glances up and sees me watching her, and gives a little finger flutter and smile.

You rock, she mouths, and keeps blending.

I feel those words all the way from my chest to my cock.

But those aren't the body parts I need to save this wedding reception, so I concentrate on unwrapping the chicken breast and packing it into the food processor.

The next thirty minutes whiz by in a blur of chopping and dicing and sautéing and trying not to notice how well that apron hugs Amber's curves. By the time we carry the food out to the dining room, the volunteer cleaning crew has managed to mop up most evidence of the great meatball massacre.

There are still marinara stains on the curtains, and some of the pretty pastel tablecloths have been swapped out for a garish orange I can only guess were left from some Halloween bash.

But all things considered, it could be worse.

I busy myself dishing up food and making myself useful. By the time I sit down to eat, I'm wiped. Wiped, but satisfied.

"These are fantastic." Amber gives me her own satisfied smile and bites into another meatball.

Is it wrong that I feel absurdly gratified at being the one to put that look on her face?

"The sauce turned out better than I expected," I tell her. "You've got mad blending skills."

She laughs and swirls another meatball around in a puddle of sauce. "That was pretty much the best wedding gift ever. I have no idea how you pulled that off."

"Practice," I tell her. "And good assistants. This isn't my first rodeo." I stab a meatball of my own and frown. "Actually, I've never been to a rodeo."

"Maybe I should take you to the Sister's Rodeo in June. It's a Central Oregon rite of passage."

"And maybe I should make my famous lamb meatballs with lemon-cumin yogurt for you sometime. They'll blow these out of the water."

Amber grins. "I'd love that."

And I love that we're talking like we'll still be hanging out together months from now. I don't know what this is between us —hopeful flirtation? Sexually-charged friendship? Something else entirely?

I only care that we keep doing it. I like the version of me that I get to be with Amber, and I don't want to stop anytime soon.

Our happy little interlude is interrupted by the mother of the groom pushing through the crowd to make her way to our table. "There you are." She puts a hand on my shoulder and stoops down between Amber and me. "I just want to thank you one more time for everything you did. The meatballs were outstanding. And the sauce—"

"I'll email you the recipe," I promise, folding my napkin and setting it aside.

Amber leans across me, and I suck in a breath as her breast grazes my forearm. "The wedding was beautiful, Mrs. Lucas."

"It was, wasn't it?"

Amber squeezes my hand. "If you like the meatballs, make sure you tell everyone you know to make dinner reservations at Juniper Fine Dining after they open," she says. "They're in the main lodge out at Ponderosa Luxury Ranch Resort."

"I certainly will. And thank you for all your help, Amber." She lowers her voice and leans in conspiratorially. "You know, I have to confess, I always hoped he'd marry you."

Amber's face goes blank. "Who?"

"Greg, of course." She shoots me a fond smile and touches my shoulder. "Obviously, you snatched her up, and that's wonderful for both of you."

"I—uh—thanks?" I'm not sure what else to say, so I settle for keeping my mouth shut and looking to Amber for guidance.

My date looks as befuddled as I feel. "But Greg and I never even dated."

"Oh, I know that." Mrs. Lucas waves a hand as though dismissing the act of dating as an unnecessary precursor to wedded bliss. "It's just that all the moms wanted you for our sons. Who wouldn't?" She seems to direct this question at me, so I nod numbly. "Always the prettiest and friendliest little girl, and so smart."

"Can't argue with that." I glance at Amber, who looks like she's hoping for another chafing dish explosion to get her out of this. What would Greg's new wife think of this weird conversation?

"Thank you for your sweet words, Mrs. Lucas," Amber says carefully. "I think Greg did well for himself with Aline."

"Oh, I love Aline." The older woman pats Amber's hand, and I wonder how many trips she's made to the champagne fountain. Maybe that's why she's acting so nutty. "Aline's just perfect for Greg, and I'm so glad they found each other. You know how it is, though."

"Um—"

Mrs. Lucas turns to me, ready to inform me how it is. "Everyone loves Amber. And have you seen those high school photos of her where she looks like a supermod—"

"I love your dress, Mrs. Lucas," Amber blurts.

The older woman nods her thanks but keeps going. "Flawless Amber, that's what they called her. And the way she'd always—"

"Yep, I sure like this dress." Amber tugs the sleeve. "Great color on you."

Mrs. Lucas frowns, but at least she stops talking. I sling my arm around the back of Amber's chair and give a supportive squeeze. "Amber's pretty great," I agree, watching my date poke a meatball around her plate without looking at either of us. "You must be very proud of your son. Seems like he chose a great girl to marry."

Amber still looks uncomfortable, and I'm trying to think of how to extract us from this conversation when the bride herself comes rushing over. Her mother is five steps behind her, gamely holding up the back of Aline's wedding dress.

"Thank God you're still here," the bride gushes, and it takes me a moment to realize she's talking to me. "I hadn't gotten the chance to thank you yet."

"It was no trouble at all," I assure her. "Happy to pitch in."

"I saw pictures on my mom's phone." Aline grimaces. "What this place looked like before you all got it cleaned? That wasn't 'nothing.' You saved the day. And these meatballs, my God—" she lowers her voice. "So much better than the ones we sampled from the caterer."

"It's a family recipe," I tell her. "My mom's actually."

I rarely mention my mother in public, and I have no idea why I just said "mom" instead of "mother." Maybe something about being surrounded by all this maternal energy.

The bride shudders. "And your beautiful dress!" She fingers the fabric of Amber's tomato-stained sleeve. "Please let me pay to have this cleaned. Both of you, please. My treat."

"You don't have to do that," I assure her.

"No, I insist," Aline says. "I've already spoken with the dry-cleaner across the street, and they promised a super-fast turn-around if you'd like to do it right now."

"Uh, now?" I have a sudden mental picture of waiting naked

in my car with Amber in the passenger seat beside me wearing nothing but her bra and panties.

I tug at my shirt collar and try to focus on what Amber is saying.

"There's no rush," Amber says. "We're fine, really."

"Besides, it's not like we have a change of clothes with us," I add.

"I'm sure we could find something temporary for you." The mother of the bride makes a tsk-tsk sound. "You don't want those stains to set."

"Tell you what," Aline says. "We have a couple extra suites in the block of rooms we reserved for wedding guests. What if we set you up in one of those, and you spend a couple hours soaking in the Jacuzzi and hanging out in the hotel robes while your clothes get cleaned."

"Or you could stay the night," adds the bride's mother. "The room is all yours."

Aline smiles at me, then Amber. "What do you say?"

I turn to Amber, trying my damnedest to read her expression. "I—uh—we—"

"We'd love to spend the night." She clears her throat and puts a hand on my knee. "Thank you so much for your generosity."

What?

There's a little more chit chat after that, but I barely hear a word of it. I'm only conscious of Amber's hand on my leg, on the ring of her words in my head. Did she just say what I think she did?

We'd love to spend the night.

The wedding party wanders away, and Amber watches them go. When her gaze swings back to mine, her brown eyes have deepened to a hue that's almost black. She bites her lip, and my heart slams to a stop in my chest cavity.

"We don't have to do anything." Her voice is breathy, but she doesn't break eye contact. "We can just put on our robes and eat wedding cake and wait for our clothes to be done. Or we can skip the whole thing and you can drive me home and—"

"No." I shake my head, too dazed to get the words out right. "I mean yes. Yes, I want to spend the night with you. Alone. With a door that has a lock on it."

She smiles. "And a Jacuzzi?"

"Right. And—uh—no clothes."

I wait for her to tell me I've misunderstood. That I'm being a presumptuous prick and all she really wants is to hang out eating pizza and watching cable TV in our hotel robes.

But her face breaks into a smile that's like the sun coming out, and her hand glides from my knee to my thigh.

"Well then," she says. "Want to get out of here?"

CHAPTER 11

AMBER

I can't believe I'm doing this.
   I can't believe I'm doing this.
I can't believe I'm doing this.

Those words loop through my brain in a sing-song cartoon soundtrack as Sean and I stride together down the hotel hallway. In one palm I grip the keys to a private suite. In the other I'm clutching his hand like I'm afraid he's going to take off running.

Maybe I am.

We reach the doorway to room 106. Sean looks down and smiles. "Here we are."

"Yep. Here we are!" I'm trying for cool and breezy, but the tremble in my voice gives me away. I try to cram the key in the lock, but I'm too amped to make it work.

After my third failed attempt, Sean holds out his hand. "Want me to see if I can get it in?"

"Uh, yep." My cheeks go hot, and I thank God Sean's looking at the doorknob and not at me.

God, I'm so out of practice.

"Here we go." He pushes open the door, then gestures inside

to let me go first. I step over the threshold and survey the room. Aline wasn't kidding; it's gorgeous.

Double French doors open to sweeping views of the mountains. To my left, a set of slate-tiled steps leads to a raised double Jacuzzi that's perfect for two. A bottle of champagne nestles in a bucket of ice on the accent table by the window, and I pick up the card next to it.

"Compliments of Comey Catering," I read aloud. "Thanks for saving our butts."

I turn to see Sean's gaze flick from my butt to my face, and the gesture sends twirly little confetti bits through my belly. Of course, the confetti is warring with the butterflies, so the result makes me queasy.

I set down the card and continue my survey of the space. There's a humongous four-poster bed piled with more pillows than I can count. I have no idea if there's something a size up from a king bed, but if there is, this bed is it.

I reach out and grab the headboard, giving it a firm shake. I don't realize I'm doing it until Sean busts out laughing.

"Checking to see if it bangs against the wall?" he asks.

"Wha—I—no!"

Oh, shit. I was, wasn't I?

I take a deep breath and turn to face him, hands clasped in front of me. "Look Sean," I start. "I know I sounded all brave and in control back at the reception, but actually, I'm kind of nervous."

"Amber?"

"What?"

He takes a step closer, close enough to touch me. When he does, it's the gentlest skim of his fingers under my chin. I can't tell if he's soothing me like a cat or urging me to meet his eyes, but it works either way. Tension eases from my shoulders as I lose myself in those green-glass irises.

"You don't have to be nervous," he says. "And we don't have to do anything at all. We can play checkers if you want."

"Checkers?"

He tips his head toward the cabinet behind us. "That wasn't a euphemism. There's a game board right over there."

I glance over at the space beneath the TV, and sure enough, there's an old-school wooden checkers set, along with cribbage and a box of brightly-painted Jenga blocks.

I turn back to Sean and take a shaky breath. "I don't want to play checkers."

"What *do* you want to do, Amber?" His voice is low, but he's not trying for seduction. He's genuinely asking, and somehow that makes me less nervous.

"I want to get out of this dress," I admit. "And you should probably get out of your clothes."

"I think we can manage that." Sean leans in, and for a moment, I think he's going to kiss me. He does kiss me, but not the passionate kind. It's the gentlest brush of his lips against my earlobe before he draws back. "Wait here."

He turns and strides toward the bathroom. I stand with my fingers interlaced in front of me, wishing I could take off these shoes. Sean returns a second later with a fluffy white robe draped over one arm.

"You take the bathroom," he says. "There's another robe in there, and you can shower if you want. Toss out your dress, and I'll hand it off to the dry-cleaners while you get cleaned up."

I nod, relieved that he's suggested it. That he's not angling to strip naked right away and jump right into the Jacuzzi together. Part of me wants that, but I'm not quite ready.

"Thanks," I say. "I wouldn't mind washing the meatball out of my hair."

He smiles and strokes a thumb from my cheekbone to the edge of my hairline. I lean into him like a cat beginning to purr, but he draws back and holds out the digit. "Marinara," he says. "And you look beautiful in it."

My body's buzzing with weird energy as I retreat to the bathroom. There's a whirlpool of emotional turmoil swirling in my belly, spinning with a mix of self-consciousness and excitement. My hands are shaking as I close the door behind me.

Kicking off my shoes, I strip off my ruined dress and crank both handles on the shower. Then I unzip my purse. Right on top is the condom Lily slipped me on my way out of the reception.

"Go get him, hot stuff," she urged with her Cheshire-cat smile.

But it's not Lily's advice I need right now. I hit the switch for the fan, then pull out my phone and dial my sister.

"Hey," she says, answering on the second ring. "Wait, are you calling me while you're peeing?"

"No, I'm showering." I stick a hand under the spray, then adjust the taps and step in, keeping the phone to my ear the whole time.

"You know, I'm not sure this is what Apple had in mind when they started making waterproof iPhones," she says. "Wait, why are you showering at a wedding?"

"You mean that's not what they meant by bridal shower?" I quip.

I'm trying for casual cool, but Jade must hear something in my voice because her next words come out in big sister mode. "What's wrong? Are you okay?"

"Nothing's wrong," I say. "I mean, the wedding was a little weird, and there was this meatball explosion at the reception, but—"

"Explosion? Are you hurt?"

"No, that's not why I'm calling." I hesitate, no longer sure why I am calling. Yes, I am. I turn so the water sluices down my back and lower my voice. "When you first slept with Brandon, did you go in thinking it was a fling, or did you think it was more?"

I love that she doesn't ask questions. Her answer comes with no hesitation, no judgment. "To be honest, I wasn't thinking at all," she says. "I wanted him, I had a hunch he wanted me, so it just sort of happened."

"Like, you just tumbled into bed together?"

She laughs. "Nah, it wasn't that seamless. I asked if he wanted to come upstairs with me, and he said yes. Next thing I know, we're tearing each other's clothes off and—"

"Okay, TMI, you can stop there."

"Well, you're the one who asked," Jade points out. "And you're the one calling me from the shower."

"Good point." I slick my hands through my hair and a hunk of meatball flops on the floor. Pinkish water swirls around the white-tiled drain at my feet, and I wonder how I went from the bold and sexy vixen at the reception to the girl who blushes at the suggestion of playing checkers.

"I don't want to screw this up," I whisper.

"How do you mean?"

"I don't know," I murmur. "Like what if Sean has this idea of who I am and what I'm like and maybe what I'd be like in bed, and I mess it all up?"

Jade is quiet a moment, digesting the ridiculous plate of crazycakes I just served up. "Honey, you might be overthinking this."

I sigh and shake my head. "Do you remember when I lost my virginity?"

"Darrin Ingstrom, your junior year in high school," she says without hesitation. "I was home for spring break and found you crying in the hay loft. I might have threatened him with a set of Burdizzo castration forceps."

"You what?" I choke out a laugh, trying to keep my voice down. "You never told me that."

"Well, you wouldn't tell me anything except that he broke up with you right after it happened. I had to handle it somehow."

I sigh and switch the phone to my other ear, then grab a little bar of soap shaped like a daisy. "He asked me to prom," I begin slowly. "I was just a junior, so it was super-exciting to have this popular senior asking me, you know?"

"Right," Jade says. "Even I knew of him, and he was four grades younger than me."

"Anyway, things got carried away in the backseat after prom."

I can feel Jade's tension snapping through the phone line. "He didn't—did he force—?"

"No!" I shake my head, even though she can't see me. "It wasn't like that. I was totally sober and super-curious about sex. I was willing and eager and probably even started it."

"So was it—bad?"

"I thought it was fine," I admit. "Good, even. I mean, I got off, which I guess is kinda rare the first time—"

"Aaaand, we're back to TMI."

Her words make me smile, even though my own are making me a bit queasy. I slick the nubby soap down my body, wondering how long I have before Sean thinks I've drowned and comes looking for me. "Anyway, I went to visit him the next day," I say. "Darrin, I mean. I wanted to ask where we stood. If we were boyfriend/girlfriend or if it was just a casual thing."

"That's ridiculously mature of you."

"Right? Anyway, he wasn't home, so I sat and had tea with his mom while I waited for him to come home from baseball practice."

"Mrs. Ingstrom? She was the student leadership advisor, right?"

"Exactly, so I already knew her." I grimace remembering the look on Darrin's face when he walked in to find his fling sipping Earl Grey with his mom and perusing his sister's wedding album.

Horror. Sheer, utter horror.

In hindsight, maybe I don't blame him.

"It was obvious he felt weird having me just show up," I say. "He was really nice about it and everything, but as soon as we were alone, he explained that he wasn't looking for a girlfriend. That he just wanted to find out what all the fuss was about."

"Fuss?"

"With me." I take a shaky breath and force out the words. "'Flawless Amber.'" I make air quotes under the shower spray, feeling silly. "He wanted to know what it would be like nailing the girl next door. The chick all the girls wanted to be and all the guys wanted to scr—"

"Jesus."

"Right. That was me, I guess."

"Oh, Amber."

I give a hollow little laugh, not sure if I'm laughing at myself or that kid. At how ridiculous it all sounds now. "He tried to let me down gently. He was all, 'you're an amazing girl, but I'm just not looking for anything serious.'"

"Ugh. Asshole."

"He thanked me for boning him—"

"Not in those words, I hope."

"I might be paraphrasing. Even at seventeen, I could read between the lines."

Jade gives an odd growl on the other end of the line. "Now I'm sorry I didn't castrate him."

I sigh, secretly pleased by her overreaction. "At least he was honest. Anyway, I should have learned a lesson there."

"What, that men are jerks?"

"No. That I have lousy taste in men. And that there's no way to live up to anyone's expectations. And—I don't know." I hesitate, lowering my voice. "Maybe that guys who get too close to the real me don't end up liking what they see."

It hurts to say those words out loud. It hurts even more that my sister doesn't automatically deny it.

"I don't even know where to start with that," she says. "All of it's bullshit, though."

"Thanks." I grimace. "I think?"

"You're beautiful and smart and funny and amazing," she says. "And as far as I know, Sean's not lousy."

"How do you know?"

"Because Brandon says he's a good guy," she says. "And if the best guy I know says that, it means something."

I nod, filing that information away in my brain as I rinse conditioner out of my hair. "And I guess I'm older now. Wiser. More equipped for casual sex."

"And that's what this is?"

I hesitate, not sure how to answer. "It's what I want it to be," I say.

My words don't sound very convincing, and I wonder if I should tell her I've never had that before. Casual sex isn't my thing. Every guy I've slept with—and there haven't been that many—I've thought was a serious boyfriend. Someone I thought I knew.

But looking back at Darrin—or hell, at the fact that my last serious boyfriend turned out to be a felon—it's clear I don't know what I'm doing.

There's one thing I do know. "I really want to sleep with Sean," I murmur. "A lot."

"Are you looking for my permission?"

I laugh and finish rinsing soap off my torso. "No. But maybe tell me I'm not an idiot?"

"You're not an idiot. Not for that reason, anyway."

I giggle and twist off the taps. "Thanks, Jade. This really helped."

"You sure you're okay?"

"Yeah. I am now."

Jade's quiet a moment. "Whatever you do, I support you. And if you want me to come get you, I will."

"I know," I murmur. "That's not what I want."

I want him.

"Take it slow if you need to," she says. "There's no reason to rush into anything."

"Except that I want to."

"There's that."

I smile and shift the phone to my other ear as I wrap a fluffy white towel around myself. "Thanks, Jade. I love you."

"Love you, too. Just say the word if I need to bust out that castration tool."

I hang up the phone. I'm a little less nervous, but I still feel awkward. What kind of dork needs to talk to her sister before a booty call?

But Sean isn't just a booty call. I know that in my heart, even as I try to convince the rest of me otherwise. I towel off my hair and contemplate pulling on my bra and panties again. They're sexy black lace with a thin layer of padding in the bra for extra oomph. They're the lingerie equivalent of gift wrap, but that's not what I need right now. I want Sean to see beyond the lace and ribbons and smiles and frills and boosted boobs.

I want him to see *me*.

I stuff the underthings in the pocket of the fuzzy robe and pull that on. The terrycloth is deliciously soft against my bare skin, and I imagine Sean's fingers tugging at the sash around my waist. The thought of him touching me, caressing me, sends a gang of goose bumps marching down my arms. My whole body lights up like a Christmas candle, and I wonder how it's possible to be this turned on by a guy who's not even in the room.

I take a deep breath and reach for the doorknob.

"Here goes nothing," I murmur, and push open the door.

CHAPTER 12

SEAN

*T*he second I hear the bathroom door, I whip my head up like a dog waiting for his supper bowl.

Realizing I look too damn eager, I force my gaze back to the *Sports Illustrated* in my lap and feign interest in an article on concussions in the NFL.

But that makes me seem like a total douchebag, and besides, I can't *not* look at Amber.

"Holy shit," is all I can manage as she walks out of the bathroom in a robe that matches the one I'm wearing. But it's a completely different garment on her, filled with lush curves and creamy skin and a sash I'm aching to tug with my teeth.

Control yourself.

My mouth has gone dry, so it takes me a second to form words. "You look amazing."

She smiles and tucks her damp hair behind one ear. "Thanks. Sorry, I forgot to toss my dress out. Did I miss the dry cleaning guy?"

"Nope, not yet." A knock sounds at the door, and I kinda want to ignore it so I can keep staring at her.

But I force myself up off the bed and grab the plastic garment bag that holds my own sauce-spattered suit. "You can throw it in here," I offer, and Amber complies. Her hand grazes mine as she drops the dress in, and a pleasant electric surge vibrates all the way up my arm. I wonder if she knows how fucking beautiful she is.

The knock sounds again.

"Better get that," she says.

"Yep."

I march toward the door with the bag in hand and spend a few minutes conferring with a fretful-looking woman who frowns at Amber's dress and mumbles something about it being a lost cause.

"It's a really great dress," I murmur as I slip her a crisp hundred. "See what you can do."

I close the door and turn to see Amber perched on the edge of the bed. Her bare legs are crossed, and her damp hair frames her face. I didn't notice before that she'd scrubbed off all her makeup, but she looks gorgeous without it. Sweet and flushed and maybe a little vulnerable.

"Hey there," I say softly, adjusting the sash on my own robe.

"Hey yourself." She swings her legs and gives me a nervous smile. "I was going to arrange myself on the bed like a Playboy model, but I felt like an idiot, so—"

"No," I murmur, coming to sit beside her on the bed. "You're not an idiot. And I don't need you to pose or primp or do anything but be yourself."

Her face tilts into a smile, but there's still uncertainty in her eyes. "I'm a little nervous," she admits.

"You mentioned that." I reach up and tuck a strand of hair behind her ears. "How about we just talk?"

"Okay." She smiles, but it's a little shaky. "How's your cat?"

I laugh. "He's great. Cranky and full of attitude."

"In other words, normal cat."

"Yep. And don't worry, I already called and made sure he's being fed."

I don't know why I avoid telling her it's my mother filling the supper bowl. Am I hiding something, or just weirded out by talking about my mom when I'm sitting half naked with the girl of my dreams?

Amber bites her lip. "Can I see your tattoo?"

The request surprises me, but I don't question it. I reach up and slip the terrycloth off one shoulder and turn to give her access.

"Oh," she says, sending ripples of pleasure through me as she traces it with a fingertip. "It's smaller than I thought it would be."

"There's something every guy wants to hear when he's in bed with a beautiful woman."

She giggles but doesn't stop touching me. "Your fiancée had a matching one?"

"Toast with jelly." I wonder if this is a weird thing to talk about under the circumstances, but Amber's the one who brought it up. I'll cheerfully chat about taxidermy or polio if that's what will put her at ease. "I thought about doing a cover-up. I even had an artist sketch something up once."

"Why didn't you?"

I shrug, enjoying the tickle of her fingertips on my shoulder. "Same reason Greg and Aline left their candles lit, I guess. It's part of me. Where I came from and what got me to where I am now."

She smiles and rests her hand on my shoulder. Her eyes lock with mine, and I catch myself holding my breath. "I love that about you," she says, and my chest tightens at the use of that word.

Love.

I know that's not how she means it, but I can't help that my brain goes there. "I love that you don't cover up the past or bury things and try to pretend they didn't happen," she says.

My gut knots up like wet sisal rope, and I realize I'm clenching my jaw. I should say something. I should say something *now*, open up to her while I can.

But my thoughts skid off the rails as Amber's hand trails from my shoulder to my chest. "Sean?"

"Yeah?"

"Touch me."

They're the sweetest two words I've ever heard in my life, and I sit there for a second just basking in the glow of them.

But a request like that calls for more than that, so I reach out and skim my palm along the side of her face. Cupping her cheek, I hold her gaze and smile. "I'm glad we're here together."

"Me, too."

I lean in and kiss her, taking my time. I mean to go slow, easing into it, giving her a chance to pull back.

But something happens when my lips touch hers. Maybe it's me, maybe it's Amber, or maybe it's something chemical that ignites as my tongue grazes hers. She gives a soft little whimper and deepens the kiss, her fingers tunneling into my hair. Her mouth is minty, and I wish I'd bothered to shower or pop a Tic-Tac. But the way Amber is moving against me suggests she's not exactly appalled by my contact.

"You feel so good." She presses her body against mine, and I swear to God I've never felt anything so amazing.

She moans, and it's like a fistful of pop-rocks going off in the center of my chest. My left hand drops to her bare knee, while my right trails slowly from her face down the smooth column of her throat. Her skin feels like heaven, softer than anything I've touched my whole life.

Her hands find their way inside my robe, and she rakes my chest with her nails. A ripple of pleasure chatters down my arms, and I stroke the curve of her hip with my palm. I let her explore, giving her a chance to get used to me. To be sure this is what she wants. Her skin smells like soap and I could lie here all day breathing her in.

"I've wanted this for a long time," she says.

"Same," I murmur, wondering if she has any idea how long I've wanted her.

Not just the Amber of my teenage fantasies, but *this* Amber. The real flesh and blood version who makes me laugh and ache and feel all kinds of things I never thought I'd feel.

I dot a slow trail of kisses down her chin, her neck, and into the hollow of her throat. She sighs and tilts her head back, giving me access to the most delectable cleavage I've ever laid eyes on.

The robe still covers her completely, and I ease it off her shoulders just enough to bare the tops of her breasts. I skim my lips over the curve of the left one, taking my time. She shivers, fingers curling against my chest as I move to kiss the top of her right breast. God, I love the sounds she makes. The soft sighs and whimpers, that sharp little intake of breath.

The robe slips down, revealing one peaked nipple, and I claim it with my mouth.

"Don't stop," she hisses through clenched teeth.

I draw in a deep breath, ordering myself to go slow. I want her so much, but I want to savor this even more. Her skin is unbearably soft, and the damp tendrils of her hair are a pleasant tickle against the back of my hand.

She shifts, and her left breast practically slides into my mouth. I devour it, unable to stop myself from tasting every inch of her. She's so fucking sweet, so hot and soft and driving me crazy with those hungry sounds she's making.

I ease her back on the bed, desperate to cover her body with mine. My hand finds the sash of her robe and I tug it open, baring her to me. "Jesus Christ." My throat is tight, and I have no idea where this sharp clench of emotion just came from. "Look at how fucking perfect you are."

She smiles, but there's something unsure in her eyes. "Not perfect," she murmurs. "Just me."

"To me, you're perfect." I plant a kiss on her collarbone and notice she's stiffened a little. "Are you good with this?" I ask softly. "The checkerboard's right over there if you're having second thoughts."

She laughs and pulls me down onto her. "I want you," she says. "In case that's not obvious."

"I'm glad," I say, kissing my way slowly down the center of her body. Ribs, belly, hip…my mouth claims every inch of her like I've been starving for years.

The instant my tongue grazes the soft dampness between her legs, she gasps aloud. Her fingers clench in my hair as I bury my tongue in the sweetest spot it's ever been. I circle her clit, and she cries out, arching tight against me. Her thighs fall open, giving me all of her. I'm mindless with the taste of her, with the sensation of Amber writhing against me, crying out, begging me not to stop.

Her nails claw my scalp, and I know she's there. "Sean," she gasps, and that syllable is like a rocket blasting through me. I cup her hips in my hands and stroke her with my tongue until I'm positive I've wrung every last drop of pleasure from her.

When she goes still in my hands, I look up to see her watching me from under her lashes. "Hi there," she says.

I smile and prop my forearm on her thigh, resting my chin in my hand. "Hello yourself."

"So was that a chef thing or what?"

"A chef thing?"

"The unbelievable affinity for oral." She giggles, looking a little dazed. "That was—that was—" She laughs again and grabs hold of my arm to pull me up and over her. "That was so amazing I can't even find words to describe how amazing it was."

"You're amazing." I kiss the soft shell of her ear, wondering if she wants to stop here. I'm okay if she does, even though my dick is throbbing like a jackhammer.

Her hand slides down between us, and for a second, I think that's what she's reaching for. I'm braced for her touch, so I'm surprised when she fishes in her robe pocket and comes up holding something square and crinkly.

"Condom." She gives a sheepish smile. "I want you to make love to me. Please."

There's that word again. *Love.* It should scare the ever-loving hell out of me, but it doesn't. Maybe that's the scary part.

I take the condom from her hand, my gaze holding hers. "You sure?"

She nods and gives me a small smile. "Positive. I need to feel all of you."

That's all the encouragement I need. I get the condom on, my whole body aching with the need to have her completely. God, I've wanted this for so long.

I shift my weight so I'm on top of her, positioned between her thighs. I'm right there, the tip of my cock grazing her warm center. I ease inside and watch her eyes go wide.

"You okay?" I breathe.

She doesn't respond with words. Just grabs my ass and pulls me all the way in. I can't help it; I groan aloud. She's so tight and wet, and I catch myself growling as I pull back to drive in again.

"Oh my God," she gasps. "This is—you're so—"

I know.

Somehow I know what she's saying, even though neither of us can find words. I've had sex hundreds of times before, but never like this. Never in a way that left me feeling so joined to another person that I can't tell where her body ends and mine begins.

I claim her mouth again, our kissing more frenzied than it was just minutes ago. I can't get enough of her, can't begin to describe how good it feels to be inside her right now.

There's a buzzing in my brain, and I curse myself for not

being able to hold on longer. I mentally recite a recipe for lavender crème brûlée to buy myself some time.

"*Sean.*"

And I know she's there again.

It takes us both by surprise, the sensation, the suddenness, the synchronicity of it all, and my God, the *pleasure*. She's arching up against me, the pulses of her orgasm giving way to my own until we both lie spent in a tangled pile of sweaty limbs and pounding hearts.

When our breathing slows, I don't roll off her. I anchor myself with my elbows to take the weight off her chest, and look down into those wild brown eyes. My heart swells so big I think it'll pop.

"Hello," I murmur, planting a kiss on the edge of her mouth.

"Hi," she whispers back and smiles.

I press another kiss to her temple and one along her cheekbone, pretty sure I'll never run out of spots on her body that I'm dying to put my mouth. "Would you believe me if I told you that was the most incredible experience of my whole life?"

"No," she says, laughing a little. "That's just the sex talking."

She holds my gaze, and there's something unsure in her eyes. Something that tells me we both know the truth.

"That wasn't just sex," I murmur into her hair as I roll off and pull her against my chest. "Not by a long shot."

She snuggles against me, spine resting against my breastbone so I can feel my heart thudding against her. Catching my hand in hers, she draws it to her mouth and presses a small, achingly soft kiss at the tip of each finger.

"Maybe you're right," she murmurs, dotting one more kiss at the center of my palm before letting my hand fall against her.

I curve my fingers around her breast, savoring the weight of it, the feeling of her whole body pressed against me. There's no other way to say this: I'm in love with Amber.

I've always been in love with her, but this is different.

I'm in love with the *real* Amber. Not some fantasy mermaid girl, but the one who makes me feel like this. The Amber who makes me my very best self. I love her so much I can't breathe.

It's too soon to say so. I know I'm a fucked up guy, and there's a lot I'm not telling her. We're a long way from discovering all there is to know about each other, and maybe she'd hit the road if I revealed it all.

But right now, lying here with Amber King, it's as close to perfection as I've ever known.

CHAPTER 13

AMBER

*T*he week buzzes past in a whirlwind of planning for Julia's shotgun wedding. Sean and I talk constantly on the phone, our conversations charged with an energy that wasn't there before. I think that's a good thing, but I'm not sure. How do you read a guy who admits he's had trouble opening up in the past?

But he does open up, at least a little. I hear about his childhood summers at his dad's ranch. He tells me about prep school and chef training and what it was like living in Paris. I tell him about growing up on a farm and how my sister is my best friend in the world.

We talk a lot, but something tells me we're not saying everything.

Or maybe we're just stressed about Julia's wedding. Sean has gobs of food prep to do, and I have flower orders to confirm, centerpieces to arrange, and a bride to reassure that her itty-bitty baby bump is totally hidden by the empire waist of her dress.

"You look amazing," I assure Julia when I stop by the bridal shop on Thursday to see how her final fitting is going. "Absolutely glowing."

Her mother beams at me, but Julia looks doubtful as she tugs at the accent sash around her midsection. "Maybe this should be taffeta instead of crushed velvet."

"I like the texture of the velvet," I assure her. "It's more sumptuous."

"You think?" Julia's frown lines soften just a little. "Maybe you're right."

"I'm definitely right. You look beautiful." I steal a glance at my watch. "I'd better run if I'm going to make it to the cupcake place before closing. You have everything you need here?"

"You're an angel, dear," says the mother of the bride.

Julia nods, but there's something heartbreakingly vulnerable in her expression. She smiles at me with the tiniest little one-shoulder shrug. "I just want everything to go perfectly, you know?"

"I know." Believe me, I know. "We'll get as close to perfect as we can."

Which is one reason I've offered to handle so many details I might normally leave to the family for a wedding like this. There's something about this couple, this wedding, that makes me doubly hopeful it all goes off without a hitch.

I hustle out of the shop, wondering if I should text Chelsea at Dew Drop Cupcakes to let her know I'll be a few minutes late. Two members of the wedding party announced they've gone gluten-free, and the groom's uncle suddenly declared he's vegan. The bride and her mom don't have time to sample all the flavor combinations for the last-minute substitution, so I volunteered to taste test in her stead.

Getting paid to eat cupcakes doesn't suck.

"Amber, hey!"

I freeze mid-sprint and turn to see Bree Bracelyn. Sean's sister waves from the other side of the street, and I resist the urge to check my watch again as she crosses to join me. Her Betty Boop curls are tucked under a knitted orange beanie, while the rest of her diminutive frame is clad in head-to-toe black.

"Cool boots," I call as she strides closer.

"Thanks. I got them in that consignment shop over on Harriman."

I'm tempted to ask why someone with more money than God would shop at a consignment store, but I stop myself in time. It is a damn cool shop.

"How's it going?" I shove my ponytail over one shoulder and wonder how much Bree knows about Sean and me. Jade and I share all sorts of intimate details with each other, but do brothers and sisters talk like that?

"I'm great!" Bree says. "How about you?"

"Really well."

"So you're boning my brother." Bree smiles as heat creeps into my cheeks.

"He told you that?"

"Nah." She rocks back on her heels and grins wider. "I had a hunch. The look on your face confirmed it, so thanks."

"Well played," I admit, secretly relieved to have it out in the open. "So is this the part where it gets awkward?"

"Not for me," she says. "The rest is your call. Flawless Amber's allowed to have a sex life, right?"

I resist the urge to grimace. "You've been in town less than a year. How do you know my high school nickname?"

"I'm a snoop," she says proudly. "Comes with the territory for women with trust issues. Sorry, were you headed somewhere?"

I'm two steps behind her in the conversation and wondering about the trust issues, but a glance at my watch tells me I've got two minutes until Chelsea closes up shop. "Dew Drop Cupcakes," I reply. "Want to sample some flavor combos with me? I could use another set of taste buds."

"Are you kidding me?" Bree laughs and falls into step with me. "I'd kill for your job."

"Isn't your job sort of the same as mine?"

"The clientele makes all the difference." She makes a face. "I love my clients, but the sort of brides we're scheduling at Ponderosa would send their personal butlers to bring them samples of cupcakes on monogrammed silver trays."

"And their personal assistants would hand feed them each bite?"

Bree laughs. "Something like that."

We reach the end of the block and the front door of a brightly-lit shop decorated in pastel hues. There's a glass case in front that's brimming with cupcakes almost too beautiful to eat. I push through the door, engulfing us both in a cloud of warm vanilla and brown sugar and a million other scents that leave my mouth watering.

Chelsea Singer comes out wiping her hands on a dishtowel. "Hey, lady," she says, leaning in to give me a sugar-scented hug. "I was starting to think you weren't coming."

"Just running late," I say. "Thanks for waiting. Chels, you know Bree?"

"Bree Bracelyn," offers my curly-haired companion as she steps forward with an outstretched hand. "Pleasure to meet you."

Chelsea smiles and shakes her hand. "You're from the family that's turning that old ranch into a luxury resort?"

Bree nods, barely masking her surprise. "That's right."

"Small town," I remind her. "Same reason you found out about my nickname, I guess."

"Ah." Bree nods. "I guess it's hard to keep secrets here."

Is it my imagination, or do her eyes flash with worry? She glances away quickly, so maybe it's all in my head.

Chelsea washes her hands at an adorable pink pastel pedestal sink behind the counter. "So are you ready to do some tasting?"

"That depends," I say. "Do gluten-free, vegan cupcakes taste like reindeer food?"

"Bite your tongue." Chelsea wipes her hands on a towel. "Everything I make tastes like little clouds of heaven."

"Little clouds of heaven," Bree repeats, looking impressed. "I could use more of that in my life."

"Then you've come to the right place." Chelsea pries the lids off several small tubs of frosting and pulls out a white-handled spreading knife. "All three of these are vegan. We've got vanilla, lemon chiffon, and salted chocolate. Normally I'd put them in a pastry bag and make pretty swirly patterns, but you're going for taste here, not appearance."

I consider telling her about my vulva cookie decorations but decide against it. I don't know Sean's sister that well yet, so I'd rather not leave her thinking I'm a perv.

I point to the mini cupcakes laid out on a round tray beside her. "Are those the gluten-free choices?"

"Yep. That's orange cream, mint mocha, and vanilla bean." Chelsea shrugs. "They weren't necessarily made to go together, but you said you wanted to kill two birds with one stone."

"Thanks for making this work for us."

"No prob," Chelsea says. "Here, grab a pen and some paper so you can take notes if you want."

"Thank you." Bree selects a daisy-topped pen and a lavender notecard, and I do likewise with mint-green paper and a pen adorned with a floppy sunflower.

Chelsea sets to work smearing each bite-sized cupcake with a generous dollop of frosting.

"Those look delicious," Bree says. "I'd apologize for horning in on your tasting session, but I'm not actually sorry."

"I'm glad for the extra set of taste buds," I assure her. "I invited Sean, but he had too much to do to get ready for the wedding."

"Glad to help."

"And I'm glad to meet you," Chelsea adds, smiling at Bree. "I hope you'll consider using us for any of your events that call for cupcakes."

"I definitely will." She studies Chelsea with an odd little ghost of a smile. "One of my brothers has a major sweet tooth. He'd love y—this place."

Chelsea spreads frosting on another cupcake and smiles. "I'd love to meet him."

I start to ask which brother but stop myself. I haven't met any of them, so there's no point asking her to rattle off names. Should it worry me that I haven't met more of Sean's family?

Bree plucks one of Chelsea's business cards from a cupcake-adorned holder and tucks it in her coat pocket, while Chelsea finishes spreading the frosting.

I don't know how she achieves the perfect ratio of cake to icing, but it's magical. She pushes the tray forward and starts pointing. "This is the gluten-free orange cream cupcake with the vegan vanilla frosting," she says. "And here it is with the salted chocolate, and this one has the lemon. See what you think."

Bree and I get busy tasting, making appropriate yummy noises and licking crumbs off our fingers as Chelsea batters up another round of samples.

"Mmm," Bree says. "I'm going to have to rub Sean's nose in it for missing out on this."

"I'm sure he's whipping up plenty of his own yumminess." Did that sound porny? I have to keep reminding myself Bree is the sister of the guy I'm sleeping with. I adore her, but I need to choose my words carefully.

Bree jots something on her notecard and picks up another sample. "He's been working like crazy fine-tuning the menu for the restaurant."

"The menu he's planned for the wedding sounds amazing, too."

Bree nods and plucks another bite of cupcake off the tray. "He kicked me out of his kitchen this morning after I taste-tested too many of his parmesan crispies," she says. "Rude."

I laugh and pick up a tiny cupcake with peachy-colored frosting. "I'm just glad he agreed to do the wedding catering," I say. "It's been crazy pulling it together on such short notice."

"I'm amazed he found time," Bree says. "Between finishing the restaurant and getting things ready for inspections and the stress of having his damn mother under the same roof, he's been working nonstop. He must really like you."

I smile and try to focus on the last part of what she said, but it's the middle part that snagged my brain.

"His mother?" I dig my nails into my palm, hoping Bree doesn't catch my confusion.

She grabs one of the mint mocha cupcakes with vanilla icing. "God only knows how long she's staying, but at least it's not with me. I don't know how Sean's living with—" Bree stops and stares at me. "You didn't know."

I fumble for another cupcake bite and force a smile. "I'm sure he mentioned it and I forgot," I say. "It's been crazy lately."

"Wedding planning pickles your brain like nothing else," Chelsea adds, offering a helpful smile.

Bree studies my face, her expression unreadable. "Sean's always been weird about his mom," she says. "Don't take it personally."

"Weird how?"

"She's a real piece of work," Bree says. "She's been here more than a month, and we've spent the whole time freaking out that she's going to file some stupid suit and try to claim part of our property."

A month. More than a month his mother's been here, and Sean never said a word. Never mentioned a family freakout of any kind.

I clear my throat and force down a piece of cupcake with the texture of cardboard. I have a hunch it's me and not the cupcake. "She could take your resort?"

Bree shakes her head and glances at Chelsea, who gives her a reassuring smile. "No," Bree says carefully. "Our lawyers seem confident that can't happen. But she could tie us up in legal crap, and that's a pain. Not to mention expensive." She shrugs and reaches for another piece of cupcake. "It wouldn't be so bad, but Sean refuses to talk about it."

The words tumble around together in my head, and I try not to read too much into this. Is it a red flag that Sean never mentioned something so huge?

Bree studies my face again, and I force a smile. "I love this one," I say, pointing to the sample with vanilla and lemon.

Hesitating only a moment, Bree takes my cue. "This one with orange and salted chocolate is my favorite."

"Mine, too," Chelsea says. "It was our most popular combination over the holidays."

Chelsea smiles at me, but there's a question in her eyes.

You okay?

I nod and pick up a sample with vanilla on mint mocha. I'm sure there's nothing to worry about. Bree's comment about trust issues just set me on edge, that's all. There's no reason to panic. No reason to assume Sean is anything but a super nice guy who's a little closed off.

I can't let this wig me out. I don't know where things are headed with us, but I can't sabotage things by worrying he's another jerk who's destined to shut me out now that he's gotten what he wants.

Dusting my hands on a little pink napkin, I jot a few notes on my mint-green index card. "I'm really liking the vanilla and lemon. Very bright and springy."

Chelsea smiles and hands me a bottle of water. "Here's this, in case you want to cleanse your palate."

"Thanks." I take a swig from the bottle, less worried about my palate than I am the lump in my throat.

CHAPTER 14

SEAN

I flip the switch on my coffee pot and glance at my watch. Six a.m.

Amber's early rising habits might be rubbing off on me.

The thought of Amber—and okay, the whole "rubbing off" thing—reminds me of last night in her barn when our final survey of the reception site turned into a whole lot of heavy breathing in the hay loft.

"I can't believe how happy I am when I'm with you," I told her, plucking a bit of straw from her hair. "You're amazing."

She smiled up at me with her cheeks still flushed with pleasure. "So was that swirly thing you just did with your thumb."

I laughed and leaned in to kiss her again, ignoring the stab of guilt in the center of my chest. There's still time to be honest. Time to open up the way I know I should. Right then, right there in that hay loft, I chose to stay in the moment, to lay her back against the straw with my hand sliding up her—

"Good morning!"

I whirl to face my mother, who sashays into the kitchen in a shimmery silver robe that looks like expensive silk. I grip the edge of the counter and ignore another stab of guilt. It's the kind that tells me I have no business fantasizing about my dream girl when there's all this other shit to deal with. "I didn't know you were up."

"I heard you moving around out here and thought I'd see if you have any coffee."

"It's coming right up."

We stand there a little awkwardly until Gordon Ramsay comes ambling out of the living room, his crooked whiskers making him look like a disgruntled mobster shaking off a hangover. His three-legged gait adds an extra swagger to his step, and he shoots a disdainful look at my mother as he passes her en route to his food bowl. I pry open a cupboard and set to work fixing his breakfast.

"Today's the wedding at the ranch next door," my mother says.

I nod, surprised she's aware of my schedule. "That's right. I'm heading over to the lodge in a minute to finish the food prep."

"Need any help?"

"I've got it handled." I fill up the cat dish and consider whether I should make an effort to accept her entrée to connection. "I could use a hand getting everything loaded up, though."

"I'm sure one of your brothers can help," she says, waving a hand. "Or Breann. Lord knows she's got the muscles for it."

And just like that, my warm feelings for my mother start to shrivel. I'm saved from replying when my phone rings. I slide it out of my pocket, thrilled when I see Amber's name on the readout.

"Hey there," I murmur, keeping my voice low. "How'd you sleep?"

My mother lifts her perfectly-sculpted eyebrows, but says nothing. Just sets to work pouring herself a cup of coffee. I move into the living room, wanting a little privacy.

"Morning." Amber's voice is tight and breathless. "The flowers are too tall for the mason jars, and we're having to trim them all down by hand. The flower girl came down with chicken pox, and we just got word that the DJ got thrown in the slammer last night for drunk and disorderly conduct."

"Yikes."

"I'm calling so you can tell me it'll all be okay."

My urge to swoop in and save the day is overpowering. But she's asking for words, not damage control. In a weird way, it's gratifying to know words could be enough. "It'll be okay," I tell her. "It may not be perfect, but at the end of the day, they'll be hitched, right?"

"Right." She takes a few deep breaths on the other end of the line, and I picture her chest rising and falling. "I have to just keep telling myself that."

"That's what matters. That he says 'I do' and she says 'I do' and they walk off with a signed piece of paper that says 'I'm in this for good.'"

"True enough." Amber gives a tense little laugh. "I teased Jade over Christmas when she'd get all stressed about the reindeer stuff. She's getting the last laugh now."

I hear laughter in the background, followed by Amber telling her sister to can it. There's no real venom in the words, and I wonder what it would be like to grow up with a family that has your back no matter what. Is that what I'm building now with my siblings? I hope so.

"I'll come early," I promise. "The food will be easy to set up, so I can help with whatever you need."

"How are your hay bale stacking skills?"

"Superior," I assure her. "I have a Masters Degree in hay bale stacking."

She laughs, and I'm relieved to hear it sounds less tense than it did at the start of this conversation. Maybe if there's time when I get there, I can rub some of that tension out of her shoulders.

The thought of having my hands on her again sends a rush of warmth through me. So do her next words.

"I can't wait to see you later," she murmurs. "Maybe after the wedding's over, you can stay the night."

"I love the sound of that." I lean against the back of the sofa, picturing all the things I want to do to her tonight. Or now. Now would be good.

"You know, I could come to your place," she says. "I feel bad that I'm always dragging you over here, and I've never seen where you live."

My mother moves past me, toting a mug of coffee so huge that I wonder if she left any for me. "Your place is great," I tell her. "I'll bring an overnight bag."

"You're sure?"

"Positive. Listen, I've gotta go get ready, but I'll see you in an hour?"

"Sounds good. Sean?"

"Yeah?"

"Thanks again."

She hangs up before I can ask why she's thanking me. Gordon Ramsay jumps up onto the couch beside me as I switch off the phone. He butts me with his head and shoots a wary glance at my mother, who has parked herself on the saddle-colored loveseat beside the fireplace.

"That's the young lady you've been seeing?" she says.

I don't answer right away as Gordon Ramsay curls himself into a donut on my lap. So much for getting up to get that coffee. "That was Amber."

Not exactly an answer to her question, but close. I don't know why I'm so guarded.

My mother blows on her coffee. "Maybe sometime I can meet her."

"Maybe." I stroke my hand down the cat's back, knowing I need to get moving. But there's something about sitting here with my cat and my mother and warm gas flames flickering in the fireplace. It's almost like we're a normal family.

I glance at her mug and see it's filled to the brim. "Did you leave any coffee for me?"

"There's plenty left," she says.

"What else is in there?"

"Just a splash of cream, a little amaretto, and some of that clover honey from the ranch down the road. I hope you don't mind, I used the last of it."

I swallow hard, eyes still fixed on the mug. "It's fine. It'll all be fine."

"Of course it will." My mother gives me an odd look, then gets to her feet with the elegance of a dancer. "You'd better get ready."

"Sure." I stay where I'm seated, stroking a hand down Gordon Ramsay's spine. "Mother?"

"Yes?"

"You sure everything's okay?"

She tosses her hair and looks at me as though I've just asked whether Santa Claus is real. "Don't be silly, darling. Things are fine."

"And there's nothing you want to discuss? About the ranch or your grandparents' property or what's happening with your show or—"

"I'll be sure to let you know, darling."

She turns and walks out of the room, leaving behind a trail of perfume and amaretto and a growing sense of unease in the pit of my gut.

* * *

DESPITE AMBER'S FEARS, the wedding goes off without a hitch. I spend most of the ceremony setting up for the reception, but I slip into the back of the chapel to catch the final minutes of the ceremony.

"True love requires two people committed to working together," the minister says, peering over the top of his glasses at the couple wearing matching scared-as-hell smiles. "What you're agreeing to today, in front of all your friends and loved ones, is that you'll show up and do that work. You'll do it when you're joyful, and you'll do it when you're angry. For better or worse, you'll do it because you love each other."

From across the room, Amber catches my eye and smiles. I smile back, my chest filling with fizzing warmth that bubbles up into my brain. She's stunning in a pale green dress that floats around her curves, and I have to force myself to drag my eyes off her and turn back to the door. The ceremony's almost over, and I have to be ready.

I sprint across the pasture, admiring the flower arrangements that line the trail from chapel to the barn. Josh, the culinary student I met at Greg and Aline's wedding, is setting up chafing dishes and making sure the food is ready to go. He looks up at me and grins.

"No exploding meatballs this time?"

I groan and straighten the tray of soup shooters. "Definitely not. These are top-of-the-line warmers," I assure him. "Are the shrimp puffs ready to go?"

"All set," he says. "Diane's finishing up the garnish."

A trickle of organ music flows out across the pasture, followed by the cheerful clamor of voices. I glance at my watch. Right on time.

"All hands on deck." I clap to get everyone's attention as I survey the rest of the crew. "They'll start walking in the door in one minute."

Ginny the bartender finishes a final flourish on her chalkboard detailing the specialty cocktails. "Aren't they taking pictures first?"

"Nope, they did that before the ceremony," I say. "No receiving line, either. They wanted to get right to the reception."

"We're all set for the champagne toast." A short redhead whose name is Carlie or Carrie finishes lining up a row of champagne flutes on the other side of the room. "Want me to start pouring?"

"Let's wait until they get settled." I look up to see the first batch of guests surging through the door. Everyone's smiling, practically vibrating with good cheer as they chatter about the vows and the rings and when the happy couple might reproduce.

I catch myself watching for Amber, hungry for a glimpse of her in that green dress.

How the hell did I get so smitten so fast?

I don't need to answer that. I've been smitten for years. Since the first time I saw her with those brown eyes and pigtails. Since the day I watched her bare shoulders rise up out of that moonlit pond.

But it's more than that now. So much more.

Now I know her. Now she knows me, and best of all, we like what we see. God, I never thought I'd have that.

I order myself to focus on food, running between the reception area and the small kitchen in the outbuilding next door. Everything looks amazing, even the bruschetta, which I was worried about after a last-second snafu with the heirloom tomatoes.

But it's all going great. Josh and the rest of the crew turn out to be hard workers, circulating among the guests with passed apps and refilling wine glasses. I make a mental note to talk to a few of them about applying for jobs at the resort once this is all over.

I've lost track of time when a familiar laugh bounces off the barn rafters.

I jerk my head up as my pulse starts to gallop. Where is she?

I scan the crowd, hands clenching into fists. *No.*

It can't be her. She can't—

My eyes fix on the familiar form, and my heart stumbles to a halt in my chest. There's Amber, smiling pleasantly in her green dress.

But it's not Amber who's making dread pool in my stomach like curdled buttermilk. It's Melody Bannon Bracelyn Buchanan, in the flesh.

My mother.

I start toward them as my heart resets itself and begins pounding in my ears. My mother clutches a lipstick-smudged champagne flute in one hand, and I fight back a wave of dread. How long has she been here?

She doesn't see me, neither of them sees me, and I consider pushing past them and going straight out the door. Just sprinting over the threshold and out into the pasture, letting the spring air fill my lungs.

But I can't. I have a job to do. A job I've obviously failed at if I've let things get this far. Guilt jabs its sharp little claws into my chest as I make my way through the crowd.

"So then George Clooney comes up to me," my mother prattles on, oblivious to her son bearing down on her. "And he says, 'pardon me, but does this relish tray have—'"

"Mother."

Her gaze swings toward me, and I see it in her eyes. Goddamnit. It's worse than I thought. I swallow hard, trying to get a grip on the situation.

"Darling, it's so good to see you." She clutches my arm and sweeps a hand at Amber, nearly knocking the plate out of her hand. "I was just getting to know your friend here. Such a charming girl. Amber, right?"

"That's right," Amber says, smiling warmly at my mother. "Your mom was telling me some great stories earlier. I had no idea you played the clarinet in school."

I never played the fucking clarinet. I take a deep breath and force myself to smile. "Can I grab you some water, mother?" The words come out more stilted than I want them to, and I look around wildly for a passing waiter. I catch someone's eye and make what I hope she understands as a universal gesture for H20. She nods and disappears toward the bar.

"Sweetheart," my mother says, still clutching my arm. "How is it possible that Amber never heard the story about that time you accidentally used salt instead of sugar in the crème brulée when you were a contestant on that Gordon Ramsay show?"

Amber gives me an odd look. "I had no idea you were on *Hell's Kitchen*."

"It was a long time ago," I say. "Before I even went to culinary school."

My mother pats my arm. "It nearly ruined his career, but—"

"We don't need to do this right now, Mother." I put a stiff arm around her, willing her to shut the hell up. To stop talking right now while we can still stop this snowball from tumbling into an avalanche.

But my mother is oblivious. She offers Amber the indulgent *just-between-us* smile she gives the cameras when she's sharing some secret ingredient. "Honestly, he's such a party pooper sometimes," she stage-whispers. "You're the first girl he's dated with spunk. They're usually these cardboard model types who look like he trimmed them out of *Vogue* and propped them up on a stick."

She clinks her glass against Amber's bottle of soda, convinced she's just paid her a compliment. But I see Amber wince, and I know I need to redirect this damn conversation as fast as possible.

"Mother." I clear my throat. "How did you get here?"

"I borrowed your car, of course." She gives a mock shudder and takes another sip of champagne. "The resort has these lovely white vans with automatic transmission, but of course they're all in use," she tells Amber. "That silly Audi is so hard to drive with the stick shift and all."

Christ. I need to get her out of here.

Amber chatters happily with a story about learning to drive a farm truck. I'm missing the details as I fumble around in my brain for a way to make a subtle, graceful exit.

My mother yanks my arm again. "I was telling Amber it would be fun to have the two of you come to one of my tapings," she says. "I could fly you both out as soon as the show starts back up."

"That would be amazing." Amber gives me an odd look, probably wondering why I'm sweating like a wrestler and clutching my phone like I expect it to beam me up. "I had no idea your mom was *the* Chef Melody."

"The one and only." I force a smile. "We've been trying to keep it a little quiet, you know?"

"Ah, the paparazzi." My mother laughs and swipes a champagne flute off the tray of a passing waiter. I start to reach for it when a woman in a pink dress rushes over.

"Oh my goodness, Chef Melody?" The woman practically swoons as my mother turns to smile. "I'm a huge fan of your show. I loved that episode where you did that thing with the melon and the prosciutto and all those little edible flowers?"

My mother swirls her champagne and laughs a little too loudly. "That was a good one, wasn't it?"

"I'm Sandra, and I was wondering if I could get a photo with you to post on—"

"Actually, Sandra, we're trying to keep things sort of hush-hush here." I edge closer to my mother, desperate to do damage control. "Chef Melody was just leaving. We don't want to steal the bride and groom's thunder, you know?"

"Oh." The woman frowns. "Right, I understand. But if I could just get an autograph—"

"Later," I say, my voice sharper than I mean it to be. "We'll mail you one, I promise."

I can feel Amber's eyes on me as the woman shoots me a confused look, then frowns and wanders away.

There's no relief, though, because my mother is talking again and my head is pounding and *oh my God* I need this to stop.

"Well, anyway, Amber," my mother continues, "it's like I was saying—"

"I'm texting Bree," I interrupt, punching her number on my phone. "I can't get away right now to take you home, but you can't stay here, Mother."

"Why ever not?"

"Because you're not on the guest list."

I type the words as fast as I can, trying not to notice my fingers shaking on the phone screen.

MOTHER CRASHED WEDDING PLEASE COME.

AMBER MOVES CLOSER as I shove the phone back in my pocket. "We built some wiggle room into the food budget," she whispers. "I'm sure it wouldn't be a big deal for her to stay."

"For heaven's sake," my mother says. "I wasn't planning to eat anything anyway. Just visit a little. Get to know your friends. Especially Amber."

They beam at each other like best friends as my mother lifts her champagne glass in a toast. "To love," she says before knocking back the rest of her drink.

Amber looks at me, clearly trying to read the situation. I'm smiling like a fucking madman, hoping like hell she can't read my mind. Hoping everything isn't about to come unraveled. Hoping even more that Bree gets here soon.

I feel myself morphing into Damage Control Sean like the Hulk ripping through his T-shirt with green-tinged skin, and I hear Sarah's taunting voice in my head.

"Try being a real person sometime instead of a robot hell-bent on fixing things at any cost."

But the situation is too far gone now for me to do anything else. To be anyone else. I'm sweating like a goddamn sumo wrestler.

"Your mom got to meet Jade," Amber says, trying to pull me back into the conversation.

"A beautiful bride." My mother is too busy waving to the bartender to notice Amber's puzzled look.

"She's kidding," I whisper. "My mother's a big jokester."

"Oh." Amber frowns, then steps closer and lowers her voice. "It really isn't a big deal if she wants to stay," she whispers. "The bride was thrilled about having a celebrity at the wedding. She asked the videographer to get some footage of the two of them—"

"No." I wave at a guy with tray of champagne flutes, giving him my best "keep away" look. The guy hesitates, then heads the other direction.

Jesus, where is Bree?

"Darling," my mother says, grabbing my arm again. "Amber tells me the two of you are very serious. Wedding bells, maybe?"

Amber's eyes go wide, and the color drains from her face. "I never said—"

"Tell you what," my mother says, oblivious to Amber's distress. To my distress. To any of the chaos around her. "Maybe Amber can come by the house tonight and the three of us can—"

"We're just friends," I blurt, needing my mother to drop this. Needing to get her the hell out of here before she does any more damage. "I'm sorry there's been a misunderstanding, but we really do need to get you out of here."

My phone buzzes in my back pocket and I almost wilt with relief. I yank it out of my pocket and scan the text from Bree.

JUST GOT HERE. WTF?

.   .   .

"I'LL EXPLAIN LATER," I say, not sure if I'm talking to Amber or Bree or myself. My heart is hammering in my head, and I spot another wide-eyed pair of fans pointing at my mother and mouthing the words "Chef Melody."

I grab my mother's arm. "Come on," I say. "Bree's here. She's excited about giving you a tour of the spa. Remember your spa date?"

The spa is far from operational, but my mother nods and smiles. "I do love a good Swedish massage," she says. "Amber, dear, it was lovely to meet you."

I dare a glance at Amber, and my heart sinks. Her face is the color of egg white, and she has a stricken expression.

"It was—um—nice meeting you, too, Mrs.—Chef Melody. I— will you excuse me?"

She doesn't wait to say more goodbyes. Doesn't meet my eyes at all. Just turns away, mumbling something about checking the wedding cake.

"I'll see you in a few minutes," I call after her. "We can—uh— talk about the rest of the catering stuff."

Amber doesn't respond. Just vanishes into the crowd, leaving a twisty feeling in my gut as I turn and lead my mother out the door.

CHAPTER 15

AMBER

I stand there staring like an idiot as Sean hustles his mother across the parking lot in the gauzy Central Oregon twilight. Stars are just beginning to prick the sky, and there's a chill in the air that wasn't there when I trailed the happy newlyweds down the grassy path to their happily-ever-after.

I'm sorry there's been a misunderstanding.

We're just friends.

I keep watching as Bree steps out of her car and confers with Sean. I know I'm being a creeper watching them like this, but I can't stop. Sean doesn't see me standing here at the side door, but Bree does. Her gaze holds mine before flitting away, but I see something in her eyes.

Pity.

"Hey."

I turn at the sound of my sister's voice, and I know from her creased brow that she heard everything.

"Hey." I straighten my shoulders and do my best impression of a chick who isn't losing her shit.

"Are you okay?" Jade touches my elbow, nudging me out of

the way of a server wobbling beneath a giant platter of cake slices.

"Sure." I force a smile. "I get it. Now's not the right time to meet his mother."

Jade frowns. "That's probably not it. He's a new business owner. I'm sure he was just freaked out about having his mom crash a wedding."

I wish I could believe her. "Sure. That's probably it. I should get back to—"

"Amber." Jade's grip on my elbow tightens, and her eyes hold mine with a ferocious sort of sympathy. "Whatever happens, give him a chance to explain. Don't sabotage this."

I nod and take a shaky breath. "Absolutely."

She lets go of me, and I get back to working the room. There are old friends to greet, groomsmen to cut off at the bar, and one sly reindeer to herd back outside after the groom's tipsy uncle releases her onto the dance floor.

When Sean reappears in the doorway, my heart stutters. I watch him march straight back to the buffet and confer with one of the servers. Then he moves to the bar, his chef's whites a bright contrast to Ginny's all black ensemble. One of the kids from the culinary school walks over with a tray full of empty cake plates, and Sean points him to the other side of the room.

He's working. That's why he's not looking over here. That's all it is.

"Amber, I've been looking for you." The mother of the bride sidles up to me and puts an arm around my shoulder. "Everything's so lovely, sweetheart. What a wonderful job you've done."

"Thank you, Mrs. Parker."

The older woman smiles and waves at a twenty-something guy in a crisp blue shirt. "Have you met our older son, Bradley?" She beckons him over, and Bradley appears at her side. His eyes are bright azure, and his dark hair is thick and wavy. When he smiles at me, I feel nothing at all.

"Bradley, this is Amber," she says. "Amber, meet Bradley. He's been away at medical school, but he'll be back later this year to do his residency at St. Charles."

"Pleasure to meet you." Bradley shakes my hand with a grip that's firm and warm and a look that says, "pardon my mother," but also "hello, there."

My whole body feels numb, but I clear my throat and force a smile. "It's very nice to meet you, Bradley. Will you excuse me a minute? I need to see if the bartenders are running low on ice."

I turn and hurry away, needing to get out of here. Needing to stay focused on my job.

"Thanks again, dear," calls the mother of the bride as I hurry away. "We'll be in touch later this week."

I force myself to do a cheerful wave before darting back across the room to where Ginny—who has plenty of ice—tries to hand me a glass of wine. "You look like you need this."

I shake my head, needing to keep my head clear. Maybe some fresh air will help.

"I'll pass on the wine while I'm working," I tell Ginny. "Can I get you anything from next door?"

She surveys the bar and shrugs. "If you have another jar of maraschino cherries, we're getting low."

"Coming right up."

I hurry out of the barn, taking big gulps of sage-scented breeze as I hurry down the path toward the outbuilding where we're keeping all the food.

Everything's fine. Everything will be fine. There's no need to freak out, to start jumping to conclusions.

I'm breathless by the time I reach the other building. Flinging the door open, I nearly collide with Sean.

"Amber," he says, gripping me by the arms.

"Hey." I glance down, surprised to see he's changed out of his chef's uniform. "Are you leaving?"

He nods and releases me. "Yeah." His throat moves as he swallows and takes a step back. "Meal service is done, and Josh has cleanup under control. I'll be back in a few hours to pack up my stuff."

I can't read his expression. His green eyes are darting all over the place like he wants to be anywhere but here. Like he's been caught doing something regrettable. Am I reading too much into this?

Maybe I'm overreacting. I take a shaky breath and offer up the most natural smile I can muster. "It was nice meeting your mother."

Sean closes his eyes briefly, hands balling into fists. "Right," he says. "I'm really sorry about that."

"It wasn't a big deal." I wave a hand, letting him know it's cool. I'm fine. Everything's fine here. "I was a little surprised to find out your mom is *the* Chef Melody. Seems like something you would have mentioned."

Shit. I didn't mean to say that. I didn't mean for it to come out like an accusation. I'm still smiling, but Sean isn't. There's a muscle twitching beside his left eye, and I know whatever comes out of his mouth next isn't going to be good. *I know.*

"Amber."

My mouth goes dry as I wait for the rest of the sentence. Wait for an explanation or an apology or some indication of what's going through his head. But Sean just looks at me, those green eyes dark and uncertain.

Give him a chance to explain. Don't sabotage this.

Jade's words force me to take a shaky breath, and I will myself not to freak out. I can't jump to conclusions here. Maybe everything's really okay.

But Sean says nothing. It's like he's lost his power of speech. Like the words he needs to say are covered in barbed hooks and stuck in the back of his throat.

Ordering my voice not to wobble, I tuck my hair behind one ear. "So, uh—are you still planning to stay the night?"

He closes his eyes again and takes a heavy breath. When his

eyes open, I have my answer. I have it before he says a single word.

But the words themselves sting more. "You're an amazing girl, but—"

"No, it's fine." I choke out an awkward laugh and take a step back. "Whatever, it's no big deal."

Sean shakes his head, hands still clenched in fists. "Things are a little complicated for me right now."

"Complicated," I repeat, nodding like an idiot. "You mean the fact that your famous mother has been staying with you all month and you never once mentioned it? That kind of complicated?"

He winces, and I wish I could take back those words. Maybe not the words, but the tone. I hate how bitter I sound, but I'd hate myself more if I didn't say what I'm thinking. If I let myself simmer on the hurt. It's like Sean clamming up is having the opposite effect on me.

Sean opens his mouth, then closes it. I see him wrestling with words, but I don't expect the ones he actually says.

"You're an amazing girl," he says again, and I swear to God I've never hated any four words more. "I just don't think I have the bandwidth for this right now."

I stare at him. "The bandwidth."

His throat moves as he swallows with an audible click. "We said from the start that we weren't going to get involved," he says. "That neither of us wanted a relationship right now."

I could punch him right now. I curl my fingernails into my palm and force myself to count to ten. Five. Whatever. "We also said we weren't going to sleep together," I say. "I guess we're both big fat liars."

The look in his eyes is almost enough to make me dial back the snark. But the words coming out of his mouth flip the switch the opposite way.

"I really have enjoyed your company," he says slowly. "And maybe once things aren't so messed up—"

"Sure, that's fine." I force a smile I'm positive looks like a serial killer's and take a step back. "Look, I need to get back over there. You have what you need to finish up the job?"

Sean seems to hesitate, then gives a sharp nod. "Yeah. I'm good."

"Great!"

Tears sting the back of my throat as I order myself to keep smiling like a goddamn Barbie doll. I try taking another step back, but my heel catches on a warped floorboard. Sean jumps to catch me, but I yank myself back and wave him off. "It's fine. I'm fine. It's been a pleasure working with you."

I start to offer a handshake, but bury my fist in the folds of my dress instead. It's not that formality would be ridiculous at this point. It's that touching him, even a little, would unravel me.

I edge back again, determined to escape with my dignity intact. That'll be a first. "It's been nice knowing you. I'll see you around I'm sure."

Then I turn and stumble out the door, gulping back tears as I hurl myself into the darkness.

CHAPTER 16

SEAN

I don't know how long I stand there in the doorway of my guest bedroom, watching my mother sleep. The blankets rise and fall in a steady rhythm, assuring me she's still breathing and is likely to wake up with a bad hangover instead of not waking at all.

That's always been my biggest fear, ever since I was little. That she'd lie down to sleep it off and would never get up.

I jump when someone touches my arm. "Hey."

I turn to see Bree watching me with concern. "I made you some tea."

"Tea?"

She shrugs and drops her hand. "It seems like the kind of thing normal families would do," she says. "Make tea and talk about their feelings."

I can't think of anything to say to that, so I follow her down the hall and into the living room, willing to swill gallons of Earl Grey if it will lend some semblance of normalcy to this situation.

Bree hands me a steaming mug and waits for me to settle into the lodge-style club chair beside the fireplace. She takes her time arranging her own mug on the soapstone coaster next to the wide loveseat the color of old saddle leather. Tucking one leg under her, she picks up the mug and blows on it, leveling me with a look I can't quite read.

"So," she says slowly, her eyes not leaving mine. "Were you ever going to tell us?"

"Tell you what?"

Bree rests the mug on her knee and gives me a pointed look. "That your mother isn't here to steal our property."

"I told you that already." My palms are sweating where they clasp the wide clay mug, and I wonder how much my sister knows.

"You weren't convincing," she says.

"And that's my fault?"

"It is, actually," she says slowly. "You let us run with that theory because you liked it better than the truth."

There's something about the word *truth* that sends a painful rattle through my bones. I swallow hard and look down into my mug. "What's the truth?"

Bree is silent for so long that I finally look up. I wish I hadn't. Her eyes are clouded with sympathy so fierce it makes my throat close up. How long has she known? An hour? A few weeks?

Maybe her whole life.

"Your mom's not a greedy bitch who came to steal our ranch," Bree says slowly. "She's an alcoholic."

Alcoholic.

That word hits harder, the force of it like a brick to the chest. It's not like I haven't heard it a thousand, a million times in my own head.

But I've rarely said it aloud. Not even to Sarah, though she probably guessed. We never talked about it, not even when she begged me to open up.

For the briefest second, I consider arguing. But there's no point. Not the way my sister is looking at me.

"Yes," I say softly. "My mother is an alcoholic."

Bree nods once and lifts her tea to her lips. She sips slowly, not taking her eyes off me as she rests her mug back on her knee. "How long have you been covering for her?"

I don't answer, mostly because I can tell she knows.

Too long.

Forever.

"It hasn't always been bad," I say. "We've had long stretches where she's totally fine."

"It's a disease, Sean. It's never totally fine."

"You think I don't know that?" The words come out like a slap, and Bree presses her lips together.

"Sorry," I mutter, raking my hands through my hair. "I just— I'm not reacting well today."

That's the fucking understatement of the year. I think of Amber's face in the barn, the crestfallen look in her eyes as I hustled my mother away. I think of how horribly I handled our conversation afterward, the stupid things I said in my urgency to escape. To get away fast before all the secrets came tumbling out like pennies from a shattered piggybank.

I've never hated myself more.

Bree clears her throat. "So you've been covering for her."

"I couldn't say anything."

"Because she's famous or because she's your mother?"

"Yes." It's the answer to both questions, and Bree knows that. "She's a high-functioning alcoholic."

"She masks it well," Bree says. "So do you."

That's hardly a skill I want on my résumé, but it's true. I'm the master of covering for my mother. King of the co-dependent relationship. *Damage Control Sean.*

Only I've failed miserably now at the one job I've done my whole life.

"I've begged her to get help," I say. "Twice she went to Betty Ford, but she never stayed more than four days."

Bree frowns and twists her mug in her hands. "Don't I see her swilling wine on her program all the time?"

I nod and look down into my own cup. The clay is warm in my hand, but I can't bring myself to take a drink. "That's part of the problem," I say. "Her whole shtick is wine and food pairings. How do you keep that going when you're not someone who knows how to stop at one glass?"

"You find another career."

"Good idea," I mutter. "I'll wait here while you go tell her that. Let me know how it goes."

Bree lifts an eyebrow, along with her mug. She takes a long sip. "Okay, so it's not that easy."

"You think?"

"Don't be a dick, Sean. I'm trying to help."

She's right, I am being a dick. I'm not used to having anyone else know my secrets. I feel exposed and embarrassed and horribly, horribly ashamed.

"I'm sorry," I whisper.

"I know you are."

Neither of us says anything for a long time. I finally take a swig from my mug, letting the liquid burn all the way down. My throat is tight and itchy, and I can't get comfortable in this chair.

"I wanted to tell you," I say softly. "So many times over the last year. Longer than that." I shake my head, hardly believing the words coming out of my mouth. They've been bottled up so long. "It would have been nice to confide in someone. In you or James or Mark or—"

"We all would have supported you, you know."

"I know. But you already hated her."

"We never hated her."

I lift an eyebrow, and Bree stares back at me, then gives a nod of concession. "Fine. She's not my favorite person." She sets her mug down and leans over the space between us to rest a hand on my knee. "We still would have helped."

"You can't help someone who won't admit there's a problem. Believe me, I've tried."

"You've been carrying this around a long time."

My throat tightens again, and I consider chugging the whole mug of tea to keep from feeling like I'm choking. "It would destroy her if it got out."

"It's been destroying you," she says. "Keeping that secret? That's no way to live. No way to build relationships."

The words sting, mostly because she's right. It's never been easy, not with Sarah or any of the other girls I dated.

But it's never felt like it did with Amber. I've never wanted to tell someone, to usher her through the carefully guarded door and show her all the battered, dingy furniture and holes in the drywall. The ugly scenery of my real life. No one but her has ever come close to seeing that.

I picture her eyes again, that flash of pain, followed by something more heartbreaking.

Resignation. Like she knew all along this would happen. Like she always knew I'd end up hurting her.

My throat is so tight I can hardly breathe, so I draw the mug to my mouth and inhale warm bergamot vapor. It's a fragrant steam bath for my face, and I close my eyes to sink into the sensation.

"Why'd you break up with Amber?"

I open my eyes and lower the mug. "She told you that?"

"No." Bree lifts her own mug of tea. "But I had a hunch, and the look on your face confirmed it."

"I hate you."

"No, you don't," she says, smiling a little. "You're just mad that you've spent your whole life glossing over the bad stuff. Shoving it all in a jar and screwing the lid on tight. And now someone shows up and dumps the whole thing out on the table."

"I panicked," I say. "I just—I went into damage control mode, and I started saying stupid shit. Things I didn't mean."

Anything to escape that moment.

Bree barks out a laugh. "You've spent your whole life playing hide-the-truth," she says. "Are you really surprised to discover you lack some basic communication skills when something bad happens?"

I frown at my sister. "Is this supposed to be helping?"

"Sorry."

I shake my head, shifting my mug to one hand so I can rake my fingers through my hair. "It's like I've spent so long covering for my mother that I forgot that's not the only priority in my life. Or even the most important one."

God, why didn't I figure this out sooner? Before I fucked things up beyond recognition.

"Your mom has to face her own demons sooner or later," she says. "Now's as good a time as any to let her do it."

She's not wrong. God, I hate that's she's not wrong. I stare into my tea, wondering if there's anything more infuriating for a brother than a sister who's right.

"It's my fault she went off the deep end," I say. "If I hadn't let her get to that wedding—"

"You can't make this your fault." Bree sets down her mug and folds her hands in her lap. "She came here because she'd hit rock bottom. You're her safety net."

I wonder if that's true. Is there a reason my mother showed up here, on my front porch, on the property that once belonged to her family?

"You've always been her safe place to land," Bree says. "You've been a good son."

It feels nice to hear that, but it's hollow praise. I want to be more than just a good son. That can't be my defining role. My defining relationship. Not anymore.

"I need to be more than that," I say. "More than the guy who spends his whole life following in her footsteps and making sure she doesn't fall down."

There's more to life than that. I had a glimpse of that with Amber, and I threw it away like an idiot.

"Your mother has to help herself," Bree says. "You can't fix this."

I close my eyes tight again, wishing this weren't the truest thing I've heard all week. The second truest thing.

"It takes work to decide you're going to love someone even when things aren't as perfect as they were in your head."

My own stupid words come back to haunt me. I do love my mother, even when it's hard as hell to do it.

And I love Amber. More than anything.

When I open my eyes, Bree is standing. She wipes her hands on her skirt, then steps closer. "I'm going to go now," she says. "Seems like you could use some time alone."

I set my mug on an end table and stand up. Bree steps forward again, linking her arms behind my neck. She hugs me so tight it's almost painful.

"Thank you for rescuing me," I murmur. "For coming to get my mother without question."

"You'd do the same for me."

"And thanks for calling me on my shit," I mutter as she steps back and regards me with a knowing look.

"Also not a problem." She offers a weak smile. "You'd damn sure do that for me."

She turns and walks out the front door, leaving her mug behind on a coaster.

I don't know how long I sit there in silence. One minute? Ten? I'm wondering if there's any way to salvage the situation with my mother. With Amber. With everything I've done wrong in this whole mess.

Gordon Ramsay ambles into the room with his tail held high, the tip of it twitching with irritation. He surveys the scene like a homeowner inspecting the exterminator's work, wanting to be sure all the cockroaches are gone. I set my mug aside and pat my lap, surprised when he saunters over and leaps onto my thighs with impressive dexterity. For a three-legged cat, he's got mad skills.

"Hey, buddy," I tell him, stroking a hand down his back. "How's life?"

Gordon responds with a rumbly purr, head-butting the back of my hand as his front paws knead my thigh like a bowl of biscuit dough.

"Good Lord, are you sure that thing doesn't have fleas?"

The cat looks up and growls as my mother walks into the room. She's changed from her party dress into a pair of velvet leggings and a long silk top in pale blue. Her face is bare, and she's moving gingerly, but her shoulders are squared, and there's not a hair out of place.

"Mother." I clear my throat and nod toward the loveseat. "Want some tea?"

She glances at Bree's mug, which has a faint splotch of pink lipstick on the rim. She lifts her chin. "That's quite all right, thank you."

"Have a seat."

I expect her to argue. She does hesitate, but eventually lowers herself onto the loveseat, arranging her flowy shirt like it's the train of a ball gown. Her posture stays straight, like she's expecting to be escorted off the premises at any moment.

"How are you feeling?" I ask.

She looks at me like she's trying to figure out the trick question. "Fine." She presses her lips into a thin line. "Fine, thank you."

We sit in silence for a moment, me trying to summon the right words, my mother staring down into her lap. Maybe she senses something's different this time, because she looks down for a long, long time.

When she meets my eyes again, her expression is unreadable. "Look, I know you're upset that I showed up uninvited, but I—"

"That's not what this is about," I interrupt. "I don't give a shit about you crashing the wedding."

"Darling—"

"It's about your drinking," I snap. "It's always about your goddamn drinking."

My mother sucks in a breath like I've just slapped her. I pretty much have. I've never spoken to her like this, not ever. Not when she showed up drunk to my high school graduation. Not when she missed the ceremony for my James Beard award, too hung over to get out of bed.

She stares at me as the big copper clock behind me rattles off the passing seconds.

By the time she speaks again, the defiance has leaked out of her voice. "I thought I had it under control," she says softly. "I never drank at all on weeknights. I kept it to a minimum on the show. But then—"

She shakes her head, and there's no need to fill in the rest. There's always a *"but then."* There always has been.

I stroke my hand down Gordon Ramsey's back, earning a rusty-sounding purr. "Is the show really on a planned hiatus for ratings sweeps?"

She hesitates, then shakes her head. "No," she says softly. "No, it's not." She clears her throat. "I've been suspended. They're talking about bringing in another chef unless—unless something changes."

"With your drinking."

She nods and looks away. "I thought coming here might help."

"How?"

She shrugs and looks down at her hands. "This place," she says softly. "I thought if I could—" She stops there, gaze still fixed on her knuckles. "Did I ever tell you about my cave?"

The conversational detour shakes me, and I take a second to respond. "Cave?"

"Here. On this property. When I was a little girl. Did I tell you about it?"

I shake my head, ignoring the buzzing in the back of my head. "You never wanted to talk about this place," I reply. "Not even when dad left it to us and I tried to ask you questions about it."

"Right." She takes a deep breath and looks up at me. Her eyes are filled with so much pain it makes my chest ache. "I suppose I didn't like being reminded of where I came from. Who I was before."

There are so many questions whirling through my head, and I don't know which one to ask first. Who the hell is she, and why did she suddenly decide to remember?

But that's not what I ask. "What cave?"

My mother takes a breath so deep her shoulders rise. Her gaze is fixed on her lap again "There's a cave on the north side of the property."

"I know."

She looks up, startled. "You've seen it?"

"We talked about using it as a wine cellar."

She laughs, but it's a hollow, brittle sound. "Wouldn't that be fitting." My mother clasps her hands in her lap, and it seems to take a herculean effort for her to meet my eyes. "I spent so much time there as a girl. I used to play house." There's that hollow laugh again. "It was just me, and God knows I didn't have any sense of what a normal family looked like. But I could pretend."

My throat gets tight as I picture it in my mind. My mother as a girl, sitting cross-legged on the cave floor, arranging her tea set for her imaginary family. I imagine her barking orders at a tidy row of teddy bears, insisting they mix the cocoa *just so*. I see her with a red crayon in one hand, drawing hearts and happy stick figures, playing tic-tac-toe by herself.

It hits me then. "You." The word comes out hoarse and whispery, and I clear my throat. "The pictures on the wall. They're yours."

"They're still there?"

I nod, dumbstruck to realize what I should have figured out long ago. "I used to look at those when I was a kid. I thought they were messages just for me."

Is it my imagination, or are her eyes turning glittery? She nods and dashes the heel of her hand against her eye. "Maybe they were," she whispers. "A message from eight-year-old me to eight-year-old you."

Or twenty-seven-year old me. How did I not catch this before?

My head spins as my memories rearrange themselves, the building blocks shifting to accommodate this new information. I'm still trying to process it, but there's time for that later.

"You need to get help," I say. "Professional help, for as long as it takes."

"I know. I realize that now. I just—" She takes a shaky breath. "I wanted to see you first. I thought that might change things. Might make it better."

"Did it?"

She shakes her head, and this time there's no mistaking the glitter of tears in her eyes. "No. I mean, it's been good seeing you."

"It's been good seeing you, too."

I'm surprised to realize I mean it. My mother looks so fragile, so broken, sitting there with her hands on her lap and a trickle of tears running down her face. I reach out and put a hand on hers, and she looks up at me. "Mom."

If the word surprises her, she doesn't show it. Just swipes at another tear running down her face.

"I'll be there for you," I say. "Whatever you need, I'm there."

"You always have been."

"But I can't cover for you anymore," I say.

She presses her lips together. "I understand."

"I'm serious about you getting professional help." There's a grit in my voice that I barely recognize. "Inpatient treatment. You stay the full term until you get better."

She gives a slow nod. "I already made some calls. My manager thinks he can get me into a place out here. A private treatment facility, very discreet. He's already started the insurance claim"

"Good. That's a start."

That's all I can ask for at this point. We're both quiet for a long time, neither of us wanting to jostle the fragile plan. This new understanding between us.

"That was your girl, right?" my mother says at last. "Amber? The one at the wedding."

I hesitate, then nod. "Was."

If my mother catches my use of past tense, she doesn't say anything.

She unclasps her hands, folding one on top of mine. As she squeezes the ridge of my knuckles, I catch myself meeting her eyes again. "You know I'm proud of you, right? Of the man you've become?"

It's my turn to force a brittle laugh. "You might want to take a raincheck on that pride. I fucked up royally today."

"With Amber?"

I nod, surprised she doesn't assume I'm talking about some catering mishap. "Yeah. With Amber."

"Are you sorry?" she asks.

I wonder if she knows about the sharp teeth of guilt gnawing at my insides. If she's felt it herself. "Yeah. I'm sorry. For all the good it does."

"Then say so," she says. "If you've hurt someone, you always have the chance to go back and try to make it right."

I snort and shake my head. "I don't think it's that simple."

"You have to start somewhere. We all do." Her eyes shimmer with tears, and she reaches across the chasm between us and puts a hand on mine. "I'm sorry," she says. "So sorry for everything."

I nod, wondering what "everything" is meant to encompass.

Today's events, or a lifetime of dysfunction. The look in her eyes has the contents of my chest unknotting like a ball of yarn that's been wrapped too tight and finally unbound.

I swallow hard and place my other hand on hers, giving a soft squeeze. "I forgive you."

We aren't done here. Not by a long shot. But she's right, it's a start. A step in the right direction.

And now there's another one I need to take.

CHAPTER 17

AMBER

"Hold still," Jade says, smearing a green gob of sticky wax on my left eyebrow. "You don't want them to be uneven again."

I snort and reach up to adjust one of the big pink foam rollers that's come loose over my left ear. "Remember that time you waxed off half of the left one by mistake?"

Jade flicks my finger away from my face. "What part of 'hold still' doesn't make sense to you?"

"The still part," I admit, doing my best not to move. "Maybe the hold."

I let go of the foam roller and clasp my hands on my lap, belatedly realizing there's something sticky on the thigh of my favorite gray sweatpants. Jelly, maybe. I can't recall the last time I washed them.

"Waxing off your eyebrow was an accident," Jade insists as she presses a linen strip against my brow and smooths it with a fingertip. It's an oddly soothing gesture, considering the pain she's about to inflict. "I swear I didn't do it on purpose."

"I know. And I appreciated that you tried to draw it back with eyeliner."

"My art skills were pretty sharp." Jade finishes rubbing the strip over my brow bone, careful to leave one edge free for tugging. "It totally looked real."

"You nailed it," I agree. "If only my eyebrows were green."

My sister smiles and sits back on the couch. "Okay, that may not have been a mistake."

"I know."

"Take a deep breath."

I do what she says, then yelp as she rips the strip off. "Ow." Pinpricks of ouch shoot through my face, and I stroke a finger over my brow bone to pet away the pain.

If only I could do that with my stupid, achy heart.

"Feels like you got it all," I say.

"After ten years of this, I'd hope we have our system down."

"I don't think I'm ready to try the Brazilian bikini thing yet."

Jade laughs. "I'd prefer to have Brandon as the only one who's all up in my lady business."

I ignore the pang of regret that Sean won't be up in my lady business anymore. There's also a pang of regret for thinking the words "lady business" in the first place, but I push away all the regret and reach for a broken hunk of chocolate bar.

"Did you try the plum jelly?" Jade asks. "That's actually pretty good."

"Yeah, I'm going with the Cool Whip this time." I dunk the chocolate into the tub, swirling it around for adequate coverage. "I'm still trying to wash away the taste of Dijon mustard."

"I really did think it was pumpkin butter."

My sister's faint smirk suggests otherwise, but I'm biding my time for her to discover the bowl of crème fraiche that's actually horseradish.

See? This is normal. I'm wrapped in the familiar comfort of home and family. I don't need a stupid man.

I glance at the bowl of peanut butter in the middle of the coffee table and try not to think about Sean and his stupid peanut butter toast tattoo. Shoving my hunk of chocolate in my mouth, I chew hard enough to force back the memory of his damned bare shoulder.

"You doing okay?" Jade asks softly.

I nod and glance back at her, wondering what she just saw on my face. "Yeah, the left one stung a lot. Let's take a break before you do the right."

"I wasn't talking about your eyebrows."

I wipe my sticky fingers on the knee of my sweats and reach for another piece of chocolate. "Sean's crew should be done with cleanup by now. Nice of him to stop by."

I hate how snarky I sound, but it's better than crying. That's the alternative right now.

"You don't know what's going on in his world," Jade says. "In his head."

"You're right, I don't. Because he never let me in. Not about his mother or his career or everything that's been happening at the ranch."

Jade glances down and fiddles with one of the linen strips we use for brow waxes. "He must have reasons for all that."

"Yeah," I choke out in a funny little half-laugh. "Like the fact we weren't actually serious after all? That he turned out to be another guy looking to nail Flawless Amber and then lose interest afterward? Reasons like that?"

My sister grabs the hunk of chocolate I've just dropped and hands it back to me. "He did see the real you," she says softly. "Not a lot of people do, but Sean seemed to."

"So what does it say that he turned tail and ran the other way?"

"I don't know."

I'm not used to hearing my sister sound uncertain, and that breaks my heart as much as anything. I swipe my chocolate through the peanut butter and fight back the tears that have been simmering all evening. "It wouldn't be so bad if I hadn't started to think he was different, you know?"

"He *was* different." Jade frowns. "*Is.* He's not dead."

"He's dead to me."

"Isn't that overkill?"

I shake my head as tears sting my eyes again. I double-dip the peanut butter-covered chocolate into a bowl of strawberry cream cheese and shove it in my mouth. "I swore I wouldn't do this again. That I wouldn't get so drunk on infatuation that I failed to notice the guy wasn't really *seeing* me at all. That I was just a piece of furniture in his world. An armchair to be hauled off to Goodwill when it doesn't fit the color scheme."

"You think that's what happened?"

I nod and wipe a crumb of chocolate off my lip. "I know it is. You should have heard him. *"You're an amazing girl, but I just don't think I have the bandwidth for this right now."*

The look on Jade's face says "ouch," but she doesn't speak the words aloud. She might as well. We both know they're true.

"He wasn't in it for me," I say softly. "Not the real me. He was in it to nail his fantasy version of me. Once the box was checked, he didn't have the fucking bandwidth for the rest."

Jade winces again, but I shake my head. I'm ready for her to stop feeling sorry for me. I need to stop feeling sorry for myself. What's done is done, and I need to get over it.

Still chewing my chocolate, I gesture to my eyebrow. "Go ahead and do the right one," I tell her. "I can take it."

Maybe the sting of it will take away the other sting. Jade picks up the little wand filled with green goo and grabs the side of my face.

"Well," she begins as she smears sticky wax along the arch of my brow. "Not that I've ever said something I didn't really mean in the heat of an argument—" She gives me a knowing look, but keeps waxing. "We can't all be perfect. But I have it on good authority that it's possible to love someone and say shitty things to them. It's how you respond afterward that counts."

I don't have anything to say to that, so I let Jade smooth another linen strip on my brow line. Her touch is gentler than it was before, and I'm grateful to her for keeping me distracted.

Is it so wrong that I expected a call? Or a text at least. Just something explaining what the hell happened.

But I know what happened. Same thing that always happens.

"You're an amazing girl, but—"

There's always a but, isn't there?

Picturing Sean's butt isn't helping, so I force the image out of my head. It really is over. We made that clear, didn't we?

"Ready?" Jade reaches for the edge of the strip.

I brace myself for the sting and give a sharp nod. "Yeah."

The doorbell chimes and we both jump. Jade gives me a hopeful look. "Speak of the devil?"

I shake my head. "No."

But I know she's right. I can feel it. The hair on my arms prickles, and I get that drunk butterfly feeling in my stomach. Sean is standing out there on my porch, though I don't know whether it's to continue the fight or apologize. Which do I want?

"Amber?" His voice calls out from the other side of the front door, sending a pang of longing through me.

"It's him." Jade makes a shooing motion toward the hall. "Go put on some clothes and fix your hair. I'll stall. Or wait—let me at least pull off that strip so you can—"

"No." I get to my feet, not interested in being pretty or perfect or *amazing*. I don't know who Sean expects to answer the door, but it won't be Flawless Amber. "I've got this."

I pad sock-footed down the steps, clutching the handrail so I don't fall on my face. Or maybe that would be better. The real Amber is clumsy sometimes. The real Amber is wearing socks that don't match. The real Amber's nail polish is chipped as she stretches a hand out to turn the doorknob.

"Amber," Sean says as I pull open the door. His gaze fixes on mine and he frowns. "Are you okay?"

I push back the flood of warmth that washed through me at the sight of those bright green eyes. Squaring my shoulders, I take a deep breath.

"Yes, Sean," I tell him, wishing like hell my voice didn't crack on that last word. "I'm totally fine. I'm better than fine, actually."

"Um—"

"Here's a little secret for you," I continue, gripping the edge of the door like I'm holding tight to my own courage. "I'm a real, honest-to-goodness woman. With faults and flaws. A whole helluva lot of them. But I have feelings, too, dammit."

"Okay, but—"

"I put curlers in my hair sometimes," I shout, gesturing to the wild nest on top of my head. "I wax my eyebrows!"

"I get it," he says. "I just—"

"Sometimes I wear granny panties instead of sexy thongs, and you know what? That's okay!"

I realize I'm shouting, and I glance up to see Jade duck back from the railing above me. Something tells me I'm not making any sense and that my sister will call me on it later.

But right now, I'm too hurt to care. I turn back to Sean. His green eyes are clear and calm as he lifts a hand to touch me. "Are you done?"

He doesn't wait for an answer. Just skims a thumb over the corner of my mouth. I think about pushing him away, but his touch feels so damn good that I sigh when he pulls his hand back.

"Jelly," he says, rubbing his fingers together. "Or syrup. I thought you were bleeding. That's why I asked if you were okay."

"Oh." Heat creeps into my cheeks. "Fine. Yes, I'm a dumbass."

"You're not a dumbass." He smiles. "But if you were an ass of any kind, I wouldn't care if you wore thongs or granny panties or went commando or—you know what? I'm getting off topic."

"Right." What was the topic again?

"I'm sorry," he says. "That's what I came here to say."

I want those words to be enough. To accept the apology and move on. But there's more that has to be said.

"I thought we were on the same page," I say, hating how small my voice sounds. "That we were building something together. But you cut and ran as soon as Fantasy Amber turned into Real Life Amber."

There's something heartbreakingly sad in his eyes as he shakes his head. "No. Damage Control Sean is a fucking asshole sometimes, but I promise you the Real Me sees Real You. He sees the bra-sniffing, tree-carving, dust-mote-fairy-chasing version of you, and he loves that version more than the fantasy one. That's the honest-to-God truth."

"I—what—?"

Did he just say he loves me? Talking about ourselves in third person is making my brain spin, and I'm not sure I'm following this conversation at all.

He must sense my confusion, because he rakes his fingers through his hair the way he always does when he's trying to herd the right words into the starting chute. "Let me try this again," he says. "I suck at communication, so this isn't coming out right, but I need you to know I'm crazy about you. So crazy that when my mother showed up, I panicked. I was embarrassed and ashamed and—"

"Ashamed?" I swallow hard, steeling myself for his next words. "Of me?"

"No, Amber. Not even close." He takes a deep breath. "I'm ashamed of myself. And embarrassed that I never told you my mother is an alcoholic."

I stare at him, not sure I've heard right. "An alcoholic." I swallow hard, pretty sure I misunderstood. "But—on TV. She's—I don't—"

Christ, now I'm the one who can't find words.

Sean finds them for me. "It's been a big secret for a long time."

"And you're the one who's had to keep it." I stare at him a moment as some of the puzzle pieces rearrange themselves in my head.

"Yeah. Yes. At my own expense, I guess." He gives a hollow laugh and shakes his head. "Hers, too, maybe. If I'd done something sooner—"

"No." I let go of the door and brush the tips of his fingers with mine. "Don't make this your fault. Didn't you say something like that to me about my ex? You're not responsible for someone else's behavior."

"Yeah," he mutters. "I'm not always great at taking my own advice."

I shake my head, chest aching with the knowledge of what he's been carrying around. "I don't know what to say. Sean, I'm sorry. I had no idea."

"No one did," he says. "I never let anyone in. It never mattered before, though. Not until I met you."

A lone tear escapes down my cheek, and Sean slips a hand into his pocket and holds out a hankie. "Here," he says. "I didn't mean what I said. About this being a mistake. That's not even close to how I feel about you."

"I thought—" It sounds stupid now, so dumb I don't want to say the words. But we're being honest now, and I owe it to him to put it all out there. "I thought you were ashamed of me. That maybe that's why you didn't introduce me to your family or even tell me your mom was in town."

He shakes his head. "No," he says. "I want everyone to know I'm crazy about you. My whole family. The whole world. As a matter of fact—"

He turns and gestures behind him in the darkness, and that's when I spot his blue Audi parked next to my truck. The dome light comes on inside, and before I can ask what's going on, the doors fly open. I blink as bodies start spilling out like it's a freakin' clown car.

Sean's mother is at the head of the pack, looking much more dignified than she did at the wedding. The champagne has worn off, and so has her makeup. She looks tired and ruffled, but stoic. She's the same woman I've watched on television a thousand times, but different somehow.

"Amber, sweetheart, I'm so sorry about this afternoon," she says as she approaches. "I swear I've never crashed a wedding in my life. I hope you can forgive me."

"It's fine," I assure her, wondering if she knows what Sean told me. That he trusted me with her deepest secret. "We all make mistakes."

Bree marches a few steps behind her, followed by Jade's fiancé, Brandon, who's followed by two men I've never seen in my life. One is handsome and lean, with starched shirtsleeves rolled to his elbows and green eyes that match Sean's.

The other guy looks like he's spent the day felling trees with his bare hands. The hem of his plaid flannel shirt flaps in the breeze as he lumbers up the steps and regards me with a curious look.

"You're Sean's girlfriend?"

I blink and look to Sean in confusion. "I—uh—"

"Yes," Sean says, reaching out to take my hand. "That's assuming she's willing to be."

"You are kind of an asshole," Bree says, jabbing a thumb at the other two guys. "All my brothers are."

"But not your cousins," Brandon interjects, giving me a wink. "Hey, Amber."

"Brandon," I say, trying to get my bearings. "Jade's around here someplace—"

"Right here," Jade calls and magically appears behind me. "Hey, guys."

Jade greets Brandon with a big hug before pulling back to regard Sean's family like it's the most normal thing in the world to have an audience of seven witnessing her sister's makeup session.

"I'm James," says the starched-shirt guy as he offers his hand. "And I apologize for the fact that my family is insane."

Bree snorts. "You think she didn't know that already?"

The big guy with the beard offers me a rough handshake before doing the same with Jade. "Mark," he says by way of greeting before turning to Sean. "Is there a reason you dragged us all out here?"

"Yes." He clears his throat and turns back to me. "I've been guarded about a lot of things." He flicks a quick glance at his mother, then fixes his eyes back on mine. "Closed off and secretive instead of opening up the way I should. But right now, I want everyone to know that I'm crazy about you."

"Oh." The ground shifts a little under my feet, and something goes gooey in my center. "I'm crazy about you, too."

"No, it's more than that." Sean shakes his head. "I love you, Amber. I know it's too damn soon to say it, and Bree's probably going to give me shit for jumping the gun here—"

"You're good." Bree elbows her brother. "Keep going."

"So, I love you," Sean repeats. He takes a deep breath, and my chest squeezes at the vulnerability in his expression. "I love the real you. All of you. And that's the truth."

Tears clog my throat again, and I blink them back as hard as I can. "I love you, too," I say in a voice that's too hoarse to be mine. "And it's not too soon. I feel like we've known each other forever."

Sean smiles like a guy who's won the lottery as he pulls me into an embrace. Behind him, Mark rubs a hand over his beard.

"Shit," he says. "That's sweet."

Bree slugs him in the arm. "Shut up."

"What? I was being serious."

James scowls at them both. "Will both of you be quiet?"

Sean draws back with his palms on each side of my face, and I swear it's like we're the only two people on this porch. In the world. "I love you," he says again, looking deep in my eyes.

I don't know why it doesn't bother me having an audience, but Jade takes charge anyway. "Come on," she says, looping an arm around Brandon's waist. "Let's go inside and give these guys some privacy."

Brandon grins at Sean and slugs him in the shoulder as he walks past. "This is where you get to kiss her," he says. "It's the best part."

Sean's mother is the last to drift past, her expression tired but hopeful. Mostly hopeful. "I'm proud of you, honey," she whispers to Sean.

She pats my forearm as she moves through the door. "You, too, sweetheart," she says. "I admire a girl who takes care of her appearance."

"I—"

But that's the only word I manage before she parades through the door on the heels of the rest of Brandon's family. I have no idea if her comment was sarcasm or serious, but I don't care now. I don't care about anything besides the fact that Sean is cupping my face and looking at me like I'm the only thing in the world that matters.

"You forgive me?" he says.

"Absolutely. As long as you forgive me."

He smiles and reaches up to skim a thumb over linen strip I forgot was glued there. "I love you whether you're dolled up in a fancy dress or covered in meatball guts. I love you in smelly bras or totally braless. I love you in perfect makeup, or with a weird piece of cloth stuck to your face with green goo. What the hell is this anyway?"

"Sugar wax," I tell him, hoping it won't be too tough for Jade to yank off my face later. "You know, this isn't how I would have liked to meet your whole family."

"Don't worry, it's not my whole family," he says. "Not even close."

"That's—okay, a little scary. And strange. And exciting, maybe?"

Sean laughs and pulls me into his arms again. "Get ready for a lot more strange and scary and exciting."

"I can't wait."

And that's the God's honest truth.

EPILOGUE

SEAN

"Shh! Quiet. You want someone to hear us?" Amber giggles, letting me know she's not that serious about the need for silence.

Since I'm hoping to make her scream before the night is through, I'm not, either.

"Relax," I tell her, pulling her down beside me on the thick wool blanket I've laid at the edge of the pond. "Bree is in Portland at some marketing convention, Brandon's staying at your place with Jade, and my brothers know better than to snoop when I'm on a date."

"A date, huh." Amber smiles up at me, her face glowing in the moonlight as she reaches across me to grab the picnic basket. "I hope you know I expect you to feed me before I'll put out."

"I'll feed you as often as you like," I promise.

Forever and ever and ever, my subconscious adds.

My subconscious is probably jumping the gun a little, but it's true. I definitely see myself with Amber until we're old and gray. It's too soon to be talking like that, but I get the sense we're on the same page.

Amber pulls a bottle of Veuve Cliquot out of the basket and gives a hum of pleasure. "Oooh, fancy. What's the occasion?"

"The occasion is the fulfillment of my favorite youthful fantasy."

She gives me a coy look and pops the top off the bottle. "You'll have to be more specific," she says. "We've fulfilled a lot of fantasies lately."

I laugh and pull two champagne glasses out of the basket. She fills the glasses three-quarters full, and I hand one to her as soon as she's stashed the bottle back in the ice bucket.

Yes, I'm the dork who brings an antique marble chill bucket on a date that takes place on the bank of an irrigation pond.

"So which fantasy are we toasting?" she asks, even though I'm pretty sure she knows. The fact that we're both sitting here dripping wet and wrapped in terrycloth robes would have clued her in.

"To skinny dipping," I tell her, clinking my glass against hers. "Which was every bit as amazing as I always knew it would be, so thank you."

"Don't mention it." She smiles and takes a sip of champagne. "I always feel a little guilty about drinking this."

"Because of my mom?"

She shrugs and swirls the bubbly liquid in the glass. "I know it was her favorite."

"It used to be," I admit. "But she's found lots of other favorites now."

Before my mother had even finished her thirty-day stint in rehab, she'd lined up a book deal for a guide to sexy mocktails and booze-free beverages. It's scheduled to release the same week her new show debuts on the Food Network, spotlighting family recipes paired with specialty virgin beverages.

"*The Virgin Chef*," Amber says, reading my mind. She gives a little grimace, then takes a sip of champagne to wash it down. "I guess the shock value sells."

"That it does."

"I'm just glad you got everything straightened out with the property ownership," she says. "That the land is yours free and clear."

"It's a relief," I agree. "And it'll be nice having Chef Melody do guest chef appearances in the restaurant a few times a year."

We sit in silence a moment, surrounded by the symphony of crickets and croaking frogs who may or may not have been checking out our junk in the pond ten minutes ago.

When Amber speaks, her voice is softer. "Thank you for showing me the cave," she murmurs. "I can see why it meant so much to you."

"A little like your family's chapel."

She smiles. "Exactly."

Her fingers find mine on the blanket, and I sit there stroking her knuckles for a few seconds. "There's something else I want to show you."

"Pretty sure I've seen it all." She sips her champagne and smirks. "I've been impressed so far."

"Funny, but no." I lift the champagne flute from her fingers and set it aside with mine. Then I get to my feet and lift her up with me. "Come on. It's just over here."

I lead her along the marshy bank of the pond, stepping around a puddle that threatens to suck the flip-flops off our feet. "Where are we going?" Amber asks.

Fingering the flashlight in my robe pocket, I smile to myself. "You'll see."

I can see the tree up ahead, its leaves flickering in starlit breeze. As we draw closer, Amber makes a soft, "oh" sound.

"You found the tree," she says, running her fingers over the faint initials carved in the bark. She turns with an expression halfway between quizzical and self-conscious. "You wanted me to see my name carved next to some old boyfriend?"

"Nope." I train the beam of my flashlight on the tree next to it.

It's a quaking aspen, sturdy and gnarled with paper-white bark and delicate leaves fluttering above us. When the letters catch her eye, Amber gasps again. She lifts her hand, tracing her fingers over the letters. "'AK + SB = 4ever.'" She turns and grins. "I love it."

"I had a professional arborist do it so there's no damage to the tree," I say. "I know that's not as romantic as me doing it myself with a pocketknife, but I wanted it done right."

"That's way more romantic," she says, dropping her hand from the tree trunk and lacing her fingers through mine. "I love that you're the most thoughtful guy on the planet."

"I wanted it to last forever."

She smiles, and I know she realizes I'm not just talking about the tree. "So do I."

Yeah, I know it's soon. But sometimes, you're just sure.

As I plant a kiss along her hairline, I see her glance at the other tree. The one with her youthful carvings. A flicker of embarrassment passes over her face, but I squeeze her hand to draw her attention back to me. "It's part of your story," I tell her. "Part of how you got to me. I'd never want to erase that."

She gives me a small smile. "Like your tattoo?"

"Exactly." I squeeze her hand. "Like keeping your flames going after the unity candle is lit."

"I love that." Amber smiles. "And I love you. So much."

I pull her into my arms, thrilled by the feel of her warm, naked body under that robe. "I love you, too."

My dream girl.

I think the words, but don't say them aloud. It's true I got the girl of my fantasies, but also true she's so much more than that. The flesh and blood version of Amber is so much better than the one I imagined.

"So," she murmurs against the side of my neck. "Tell me how it went in your fantasies."

"What do you mean?"

She draws back from our embrace, and the smile she gives me sends a jolt of lust through me. "Well, I step out of the pond without a stich of clothing on," she says. "And you're up there on the balcony…"

"Ignoring the fact that my father is down here yelling at you for trespassing?"

"Ignoring that," she says. "We're rewriting our own version of the story here."

And I'm so damn grateful for that I could burst. Amber smiles and stretches up to kiss the edge of my jaw. It's a soft kiss and so light it's almost chaste, but there's nothing chaste about the surge that bolts through me. "So," she whispers. "Tell me how it goes from there."

I smile and draw her to me, leaning down to claim her mouth. I kiss her hard and deep and so passionately we have to lean back against the tree to keep from toppling.

When I draw back, we're both breathless. I reach up and brush a damp tendril of hair off her face. "How about I show you instead?"

Amber grins and presses her body against mine, the front of her robe parting just enough to leave my mouth watering.

"Perfect," she whispers. "That's the best kind of story."

***

Ready for Bree and Austin's story? That's next in the Ponderosa Resort Romantic Comedy Series, and it's a 2019 RITA Award finalist. You can get your mitts on *Sergeant Sexypants* right here:

Sergeant Sexypants
https://books2read.com/b/mqZnx8
Keep reading for a sneak peek from *Sergeant Sexypants* . . .

YOUR EXCLUSIVE SNEAK PEEK AT
SERGEANT SEXYPANTS

AUSTIN

"*I*t really would be your most noble, heroic act."

Mrs. Sampson beams and adjusts the glasses perched halo-style in her salt-and-pepper perm, then folds her hands on the bistro table like she's delivered the closing argument in a murder trial.

I fix her with my best cop stare, which loses some impact since I'm holding a plate of shrimp puffs. "I rescued your cat off the roof two weeks ago, Mrs. S," I remind her, ignoring the fact that my job also involves chasing down the occasional bad guy. "But *this* would be my most heroic act?"

She nods like I've finally gotten a question right on an algebra test, which is fitting since she was my middle school math teacher. She lifts her glass of champagne, sloshing some into the manicured grass. "Exactly," she says. "It means so much to the children."

I take a calming breath and remind myself she's an old lady. An old lady who just stroked my bicep, but still an old lady.

"Taking off my shirt means so much to the children." I set down my plate and try the cop stare again. This time, she blushes.

"It's for charity," she says. "People love those calendars that

have pictures of real policemen with their clothes off and something covering up their—" she clears her throat dramatically,
"—*unmentionables.*"

Good God, we need a subject change. "If you're mentioning
the unmentionables, haven't we already defeated the purpose?"

She ignores me and squeezes my bicep again. "You'd be
perfect for January, sweetheart, with those pretty blue eyes, and
maybe you'd pose shirtless on a dogsled with no pants but your
police hat over your—"

"Okay, no." I brace my hands on the table. "The department
has policies about police officers being photographed in
uniform." Admittedly, I don't remember a code about not using
one's peaked cap to cover one's junk, but that's beside the point.
"Following the rules is kinda my job, Mrs. Sampson."

She looks at me like I've just announced a fondness for rolling
naked in lime Jell-O and gives a sad little head shake. "You're in
line to become the next chief of police," she says slowly, like I
might have forgotten. "Don't you *make* the rules?"

I open my mouth to explain that my promotion from sergeant
to lieutenant is no guarantee I'll be head honcho when the chief
retires, even though everyone's acting like it's a foregone conclu-
sion. Before I get a word out, my father strides over in his sheriff's uniform and claps me on the shoulder while turning his
election-year grin on Mrs. Sampson.

"Judy," he says. "You're looking radiant."

"Thank you, John," she says, preening. "Would you please tell
your son to take his clothes off for the children?"

My father frowns and rubs a hand over his chin. "Well, I can't
rightly suggest that as a good career move, but—"

"For charity," she interrupts, increasingly impatient.

I fight the urge to roll my eyes, wondering what was coming
after my father's "but." Is there a situation in which he'd advise
me to get naked for minors?

Mrs. Sampson is still prattling on about the charity calendar, so I tune them out and start surveying the crowd. There must be a hundred people milling around the expansive lawn at Ponderosa Luxury Ranch Resort on this warm fall afternoon. Some of them linger by the fire pits, laughing in sundresses and swirls of wood smoke, while others chatter by the buffet tables, pretending it's totally in their normal wheelhouse to eat herbed squash confit made by a famous Michelin-starred chef.

Most are faces I recognize, all here to celebrate the opening of this fancy new playground for the wealthy. Not that I'm complaining. It's great for the local economy and all, but I feel weird hobnobbing at an event meant for VIPs and dignitaries and other local elite.

I'm hardly a VIP, but the uniform and job title nabbed me the invitation, so here I am. I pick up a shrimp puff and shove it in my mouth as my father interrupts my reverie.

"Don't you think so, son?"

I turn back to him, debating whether to bluff or come clean that I lost track of the conversation. "What's that, dad?"

My father smiles like I passed some kind of test, and I'm betting he read my mind. He knows I don't have it in me to bluff, which isn't a bad thing. My straight-shooting, rule-abiding approach to life makes me a damn good cop.

"Just saying that the Ryan Zonski case stands a good chance of being overturned if it ends up going before the Oregon Court of Appeals," he says. "You'd be right in the thick of it again."

I resist the urge to grit my teeth at the prospect of having my worst case reopened. "Let's hope not," I offer mildly. "The new DA loves settling out of court. I'd hate to see the victim's family go through that again."

Mrs. Sampson gives a sad little head shake. "Such an awful tragedy."

I'm wracking my brain for a good subject change when an angel glides into my line of sight.

She's making a beeline for us, this angel with dark curls and wide green eyes. She can't be more than five feet tall, but there's a fierceness in her expression suggesting she'd cheerfully junk-punch anyone who crossed her. It's an interesting contrast to the bright smile she offers as she approaches our table in a slim blue dress that hugs her curves. I do my best not to stare, but holy marshmallows, she's stunning.

"Marshmallows?" She looks at me and cocks her head.

Oh shit. Did I say that out loud?

"I—uh—"

"I'd love one." My father reaches for her, and I consider elbowing him in the ribs when I see she's clutching a fistful of skewers. Each one is threaded with a massive, pillowy marshmallow that looks homemade. Not that I know what a home-made marshmallow looks like, but these aren't the Jet-Puffed confections of my Boy Scout years.

"You'll find homemade graham crackers and Maison Pierre Marcolini chocolates on trays beside all the fire pits," she adds, brushing a dark curl from her forehead. "Help yourself to anything you need to make the perfect s'mores."

Good Lord, she has a beautiful mouth. That's never been the first thing I've noticed in a woman, but I can't stop staring at hers. Those lush, rosebud lips that look softer than—than—okay, I was going to say marshmallows again, which means she's zapped most of the vocabulary from my brain.

Her gaze shifts to mine and locks, and I swear she just read my thoughts. I can't tell whether she's intrigued or annoyed, but the wheels are turning in her head.

I stick out my hand. "Sergeant Austin Dugan, Bend PD."

There's a moment of awkwardness when she's forced to shift the fistful of skewers to her left hand, but the instant her palm slides against mine, a flame bursts in the center of my chest. I won't need a fire pit to turn this marshmallow to a puddle of goo.

"Bree Bracelyn," she says. "I'm the Vice President of

Marketing and Events for Ponderosa Resort. Thank you so much for joining us."

"My pleasure." The word *pleasure* rolls off my tongue with a more porny tone than I intended, or maybe that's all in my head. I haven't released her hand yet, so I should probably do that.

The instant I let go, my father extends his own handshake. "John Dugan, I'm the sheriff out here." My dad gives Bree's hand a few pumps before nudging me with his elbow. "My boy is being modest. He's getting promoted this week from sergeant to lieutenant and is on track to be the youngest police chief in the town's history."

"All right, enough." I should probably appreciate my dad's boasting on my behalf, but Bree isn't exactly falling over herself with cop worship. "This is Joan Sampson, president of the Deschutes Children's Welfare Society. A pillar of the community."

Mrs. Sampson beams and holds out her hand. "Also a retired teacher," she says, clutching Bree's hand in a grandmotherly grasp that almost makes me wonder if I imagined her badgering me to get naked. "It's lovely to meet you."

"You, too, ma'am." Bree's posture is perfect, and her manners suggest some fancy East Coast finishing school. Or maybe I read that in the paper, back when they profiled the family behind the development of Ponderosa Resort. "I'm so honored to have you with us."

"This place is incredible," I say, relieved we've moved past the subject of my career. "It's my first time making it out here."

"Thank you." Bree smiles wider, those lush lips parting just a little. I wonder if I'm the only one who just felt all the air leave his lungs. "My brothers and I have been working nonstop on the place since our father passed away eighteen months ago," she says. "We think he'd be proud of how we've transformed it."

"Your father was Cort Bracelyn." My father nods. "Helluva guy."

Is it my imagination, or did Bree's smile just wobble? But she rallies, pushing up the corners of her mouth to keep her expression cheerful. "Right," she says. "Yes. My father was—He didn't spend that much time out here."

My own father doesn't take the hint that maybe Bree would prefer not to make small talk about her dead dad. "He might not have been a regular resident, but he paid good wages to the guys running the ranch," he says. "We had a little dustup out here maybe eight years ago when some of his horses got loose and trampled a neighbor's fence. Your daddy was quick to pay retribution."

Bree's smile is tight. "He was always very generous with his money."

I don't know why, but I'm filled with a powerful urge to rescue her. To redirect this conversation I'm pretty sure she'd rather not have. "How are you liking Central Oregon?" I ask.

I sound like a lame caricature of a cop on a children's program, but Bree turns to me with thinly-disguised relief. "I love it out here," she says. "The people are so friendly, and I love seeing all the stars at night. And the coyotes—I hear them howling every night when I'm in bed."

My brain veers dangerously at the thought of Bree lying in bed with a thin sheet tracing the contours of those delectable curves, but I manage to hold it together. "I've always loved coyote singing, too," I admit. "That, and rain on a metal roof."

"I've hardly ever seen it rain out here," she says.

"That's why it's great. There's nothing like the smell of rain in the high desert. Ozone and sage and that herbal smell of wet juniper. Some of my favorite things in the world."

Her eyes hold mine, and I can tell she's imagining it. The patter of raindrops on the roof, the cinnamon scent of damp ponderosa bark, the rumble of thunder over the hills, my fingers in her hair as I tip her head back and—

"Austin has a pet coyote." My dad nudges me with his elbow, jarring me out of my fantasy.

Bree blinks. "A pet coyote?"

"She's a hybrid, actually," I say. "A coydog."

Bree tilts her head to look at me. "They're legal to have as pets?"

"Yes," I say a little too sharply. "I researched the hell out of the laws after I found her wandering in the Oregon Outback. The county regulations are looser than what I'd have to follow if I lived in the city limits."

My father laughs and claps me on the shoulder. "Austin's a stickler for the rules. Speaking of which…" He leans in close like he's got a big secret, and Bree's breast brushes my arm as she leans across me to hear him. It takes every ounce of strength I have to step back and break contact.

"With wildfire season still going strong, there's a ban on all open fires right now for public and private lands," he says. "We can let it slide since the ban gets lifted next week and you seem to have everything under control, but I thought you should know."

"Oh." Bree's cheeks go pink as she straightens up and looks my father in the eye. "I'm so sorry, I had no idea—we can put out the fire pits right now."

"Now don't you go worrying about it," he says with his *aw-shucks* smile. "Outside of town like this, and with all those fire extinguishers you've got lined up, we can make an exception. Besides, this hasn't been a bad fire year. It's really more of a suggestion than anything."

But Bree shakes her head, looking around like she expects a pair of deputies to dart out from behind the gazebo and slap the cuffs on her. "We want to follow the law out here." She looks at me when she says this, and I could swear she stands up a little straighter. "I believe in doing everything by the book. The laws exist for a reason, and I'm not one to break them."

Is it wrong that whole speech kinda turned me on?

But for some reason, I get the sense she's putting on an act. Most folks lace up their goody two shoes when they talk to cops, but hers don't fit quite right. There's something *off* in those pretty green eyes.

Bree clears her throat and looks back at my dad. "I should get back to the party," she says. "But don't worry; I'll have one of my brothers put the fires out right away."

"It's really not necessary," my father says. "But if it'll make you feel better—"

"It will." She smiles and takes a step back. "I always feel better when I'm doing the right thing."

She keeps edging away, like she's not quite ready to turn her back on us. When she finally does, I'm distracted by the wind flipping the hem of her dress, but I can't help noticing how she darts across the lawn like her feet caught fire.

I watch her go, admiring her curves, the fiery glint of sunlight in her dark curls, the daintiness of her calves, and I think I'd give anything to know what the hell makes Bree Bracelyn tick.

***

Want to keep reading? Nab *Sergeant Sexypants* here now:
Sergeant Sexypants
https://books2read.com/b/mqZnx8

DON'T MISS OUT!

Want access to exclusive excerpts, behind-the-scenes stories about my books, cover reveals, and prize giveaways? Not only will you get all that by subscribing to my newsletter, but I'll even throw you a **FREE** short story featuring a swoon-worthy marriage proposal for Sean and Amber from *Chef Sugarlips*.

Get it right here.

http://tawnafenske.com/subscribe/

ACKNOWLEDGMENTS

Great big gobs of thank yous, hugs, and awkward butt pats to Fenske's Frisky Posse for being the most amazing street team a girl could hope for. You ladies rock!

Endless thanks to Kait Nolan for showing me the self-pub world isn't as scary as I thought it was. It's still scary, so thank you for petting my hair and soothing me with wine.

I couldn't do this without Linda Grimes, who never bats an eyelash at my last-minute pleas for critiques and advice. I love you almost as much as I love your books (so where's the next one?!)

Meah Meow, I'm soooooo thankful for that day a year ago when you noticed my yelp for help and said, "I can be an author assistant!" You are amazing at it, and an equally awesome pet sitter, so thank you for both!

I'm hugely thankful to Susan Bischoff and Lauralynn Elliott of The Forge for all your hard work whipping this bad boy into shape. It finally has a title!

Thank you to all my Facebook pals for pitching in with your wedding fiasco stories. I'm especially grateful to thank Judah McAuley, Sharon Slick Reads, Sierra Newburn, Dawn Alexander, Kathy Owen, and Terri Lynn Coop. Thanks especially to Bryan Thomas Schmidt for the title idea!

Love and gratitude to my family, Aaron "Russ" Fenske and Carlie Fenske, and Dixie and David Fenske for always being there. Thanks also to Cedar and Violet for being pretty kickass step-kids. Don't say kickass.

And thank you always to Craig for being my rock, and for always believing in me. And for naked stuff.

ABOUT THE AUTHOR

When Tawna Fenske finished her English lit degree at 22, she celebrated by filling a giant trash bag full of romance novels and dragging it everywhere until she'd read them all. Now she's a RITA Award finalist, USA Today bestselling author who writes humorous fiction, risqué romance, and heartwarming love stories with a quirky twist. Publishers Weekly has praised Tawna's offbeat romances with multiple starred reviews and noted, "There's something wonderfully relaxing about being immersed in a story filled with over-the-top characters in undeniably relatable situations. Heartache and humor go hand in hand."

Tawna lives in Bend, Oregon, with her husband, step-kids, and a menagerie of ill-behaved pets. She loves hiking, snowshoeing, standup paddleboarding, and inventing excuses to sip wine on her back porch. She can peel a banana with her toes and loses an average of twenty pairs of eyeglasses per year. To find out more about Tawna and her books, visit www.tawnafenske.com.

ALSO BY TAWNA FENSKE

The First Impressions Series

The Fix Up

The Hang Up

The Hook Up

The List Series

The List

The Test

The Last

Schultz Sisters Mysteries

Getting Dumped

The Great Panty Caper (novella)

Standalone novellas and other wacky stuff

Going Up (novella)

Eat, Play, Lust (novella)

CPSIA information can be obtained
at www.ICGtesting.com
Printed in the USA
FSHW022041091219
64922FS

9 781718 732827